Beyond *the* Scans

Healing Hands, Hopeful Hearts

Beyond the Scans

Healing Hands, Hopeful Hearts

DR. MEENU WALIA

PRABHAT
PRAKASHAN

Published by
PRABHAT PRAKASHAN PVT. LTD.
4/19 Asaf Ali Road,
New Delhi-110 002 (INDIA)
e-mail: prabhatbooks@gmail.com

ISBN 978-93-5562-160-3
BEYOND THE SCANS: HEALING HANDS, HOPEFUL HEARTS
by Dr. Meenu Walia

Edition
First, 2024

Price
₹ 400 (Rupees Four Hundred Only)

Printed at
S. S. Japan Arts, Delhi

Foreword

It is an honour to write the foreword for this exceptional book by Dr. Meenu Walia, a visionary oncologist with over 30 years of experience, having treated more than 100,000 patients across diverse backgrounds. Her dedication goes far beyond treating cancer—she understands its profound impact on patients and families. Dr. Walia's commitment includes clinical work, community awareness, screenings and public initiatives. This book reflects her relentless pursuit of better outcomes and her deep compassion.

Dr. Walia shares real-life stories of cancer survivors, highlighting their resilience and strength. These are not just tales of survival, but stories of thriving against all odds, with individuals emerging as warriors who have redefined their lives through triumphs over cancer. The book blends inspiring narratives with practical advice, offering a beacon of hope for patients facing the challenges of treatment.

Dr. Walia's holistic yet aggressive approach emphasizes not just cutting-edge medical care but also patient empowerment. Her work in oncology exemplifies her belief that every individual deserves the chance to fight, with the right support enabling them to emerge victorious. As I read, I was moved by the strength of the individuals featured and by Dr. Walia's expertise and guidance, which create a powerful and inspiring narrative.

This book is more than just a guide; it is a source of inspiration and knowledge. I encourage all readers—patients, caregivers, and healthcare professionals alike—to engage with it. It is a testament to Dr. Walia's dedication and a vital resource for anyone touched by cancer.

Ms. Mahima Chaudhry
Film Actress and Cancer Warrior ❑

Author's Note

Cancer is not just a disease; it is a journey—a journey fraught with challenges, uncertainties, and profound emotional upheavals. For those who face it, cancer reshapes lives, not only altering the course of one's physical health but also stirring the deepest realms of the human spirit. As an oncologist, I have walked alongside countless individuals on this journey, witnessing their courage, resilience, and the battles they fight, both seen and unseen.

This book is a reflection of that journey, an attempt to shed light on the multifaceted world of oncology from the perspective of a clinician who has been in the trenches. But it is more than just a medical discourse—it is a compassionate exploration of the emotional and psychological landscapes that both patients and their families traverse. In these pages, you will find a blend of clinical insights, personal experiences, and inspirational stories, all woven together to offer a holistic understanding of what it means to confront cancer.

The chapters are organized to guide you through the emotional rollercoaster that accompanies a cancer diagnosis, dispel common myths that often cloud judgment, and provide practical advice on navigating the complexities of treatment. We delve into the integrative approaches that consider the mind-body connection, highlighting the importance of nurturing the whole person—not just targeting the disease. And as we move through these narratives, you will meet extraordinary individuals—survivors whose stories of remission and perseverance will inspire and uplift.

This book is for anyone touched by cancer—patients, caregivers, medical professionals, and those simply seeking to understand this formidable foe better. It is a testament to the human spirit's resilience and a reminder that, even in the darkest most dismal moments, there is hope, healing, and a possibility for a future beyond cancer.

As you turn these pages, may you find solace, strength, and the knowledge that you are not alone on this journey.

❑

Acknowledgements

Writing this book has been a deeply personal journey, and I am immensely grateful to those who have walked alongside me, providing support, encouragement, and inspiration at every step.

First and foremost, I would like to express my deepest gratitude to "The Almighty God", for everything that I have today and have been able to achieve.

My deepest gratitude to my late father Mr. G. S. Walia, whom I lost a few months ago. Your words have always been the quiet voice of reason that have guided all my decisions and choices in life. You will always be my guiding light in this life and beyond.

To my beloved husband, Mr. H.S. Bedi, your unwavering support has been my foundation. You have been my anchor, especially during the most challenging times. I am truly blessed to have you by my side.

To my son Praneet, you are my greatest blessing, I must have done something really good in my past life to deserve a son like you. Watching you grow into the remarkable person you are today... fills my heart with tremendous pride and joy. I hope that through this work, I can impart to you the values of empathy, resilience, and the power of knowledge.

A very special thanks to all my patients and their caregivers, whose stories form the heart and soul of this book. Your courage, resilience, and determination are not only inspiring but also serve as my daily motivation. It is an honour to be part of your journey, and I am profoundly grateful for the trust you have placed in me. Your experiences have enriched my understanding of what it truly means to battle cancer, and for that, I am forever indebted.

A special acknowledgement goes to Ms Saheli, an enthusiastic member of my team, whose dedication and assistance in writing this book has been invaluable. Your perseverance and deep commitment have helped bring this project to fruition. Thank you for being a steadfast partner in this endeavour.

Lastly, to everyone who has been part of this journey, whether through words of encouragement, a listening ear, or simply being there— I am most thankful. This book is as much yours as it is mine, and I hope it serves as a beacon of hope and understanding for all, who read it.

❑

Contents

PART–I

Navigating the Emotional Rollercoaster: Insights from an Oncologist

As oncologists, we are trained to provide compassionate care to our patients. We often develop deep connections with our patients and their families, witnessing their struggles, hopes, and fears. In my three decades of practice, I have witnessed firsthand, the wide range of emotions that patients experience throughout their cancer journey. This emotional involvement does create a rollercoaster of empathy, as we genuinely care about our patients' well-being.

Sitting across the other side of the table, we are responsible for delivering both good, bad and challenging news to the patients. While we strive to provide hope and encouragement along with being realistic about the prognosis and treatment options, striking the right balance between optimism and honesty can be emotionally demanding.

The demands of being an oncologist, dealing with complex cases, and maintaining a high level of patient care often leads to significant personal stress. Long hours, heavy workloads, and the weight of responsibility does take a toll on our emotional well-being as well.

But despite all the emotional challenges, most of us find profound fulfilment and purpose in our work. We are blessed that we have this gratifying opportunity to make a difference in patients' lives, witnessing success stories, and providing comfort and support during difficult and stressful times.

I read this somewhere and strongly resonate with the notions that, *"A doctor is a student till he/she dies, once he/she considers himself not a student anymore, the doctor inside him dies. Medicine is a continuous learning experience and you will never stop learning and researching new ideas and inventions for the sake of humanity."* Oncologists constantly strive to stay updated with the latest research and treatment options in the field of oncology. The pursuit of knowledge and the desire to provide the best possible care for out patients can be emotionally rewarding and keeps us motivated.

However, despite the advancements in cancer treatment, we frequently face the reality of losing many patients to the disease. Witnessing the suffering and eventual loss of patients is emotionally draining and can lead to feelings of grief, sadness, and a sense of personal responsibility.

But each day, when we begin, we have a great desire to change the course of the disease for patients with cancer; cure where possible and when a cure is not possible, to extend and improve the quality of remaining life. People say oncology is such a pessimistic field, but then what keeps me going? It is the incredible power of the human spirit I see daily – the will to take adversities head on. I have witnessed so many shades of human behaviour, and the ways different people deal with this disease differently. My patients and their undying will power is my biggest motivation that strives me to work harder and harder each day. ❑

CHAPTER-1

Diving Deep into Why I Chose to Become an Oncologist?

It was a time of profound happiness. And of sorrow. April 19, 1998. I was to get married that day, but early in the morning, my to-be mother-in-law, a cancer patient, was rushed to the emergency ward at AIIMs. Everything was thrown into a turmoil. But she was a strong lady. She insisted that the marriage should be solemnized; though she could not attend, few things were more heart-rending for a traditional Punjabi lady...

She died 4 months later.

This was my first brush with cancer, up close. I was deeply shaken. But as destiny would have it, not long afterwards, my mother too was detected with breast cancer stage 3. I was devastated. I was further shocked to realize that there was a grave lack of cancer care in Delhi. At that time, the Tata Memorial Hospital in Mumbai was the Mecca-Medina of cancer patients who had little choice but to travel all the way to avail quality care.

I remember those days... In the late evening, after work, I would travel daily from Noida to Karol Bagh, where my mother lived, to be with her and take care of her. I was the only doctor in the family. Several nights I stayed over, and next day, I made the long drive back to Noida. It was a traumatic time.

Did cancer change my life? Yes. In fact, it transformed my life. I became an oncologist with a deep understanding of what cancer means to the patient and equally, to the caregiver. Looking back at my life till then, I realized I was never an ambitious person. I would have settled down to a regular physician's schedule at a government hospital and made a comfortable life with my son and husband. But my mother-in-law's death and then my mother's brush with cancer, changed my perspective on life forever.

Providing the best possible care – clinically, mentally, and emotionally – became my life's mantra – yes sometimes even at the cost of my family. My young son often resented me for not being there for him even when he was ill... Today, he understands my calling.

I believe cancer patients have two lives – one before cancer where they lived life taking it for granted – and one after cancer when the very act of drawing breath fills one with joy and gratitude. It is like waking to a fantastic new dawn where you see the colours for the first time. My journey as a caregiver was equally eye-opening for me – it was as if I was seeing life for the first time – through a completely different prism. Oncology is no longer a profession for me. It is a passion which changed my existence.

❑

CHAPTER-2

Breaking 'THE NEWS': One Size Doesn't Fit All

One of the most difficult parts of the whole process of treatment is to let the patient and their families know about Cancer. Communication is extremely crucial between every doctor and patient, but the word "Cancer" without a second thought resonates trauma making communication all the more complicated.

The dialogue involves a plethora of emotions such as empathy, sympathy, firmness, courage, hope, doubt, shock, anger, sorrow; one emotion imbalances and the whole dialogue could fall apart. As doctors, we have to empathize with our patients but at the same time not lose our cautiousness and get driven away by emotions. But it is the same formula that works for every counselling session? No!

Patients coming from different societal backgrounds, situations, responsibilities tend to have different reactions. In the Western countries, a physical approach of holding hands or hugging the patient is quite normal to ease the patient but in India people are not so comfortable with such gestures. So how do we console such patients?

Common practice is to follow the SPIKES protocol for delivering the bad news, where SPIKES stands for:

S- Setting up the interview

P- Assessing the patient's perception

I- Obtaining the patient's invitation

K- Giving or imparting knowledge and information to the patient

E- Addressing the patient's emotions with empathetic responses

S- Strategy and summary

The protocol remains the same but the approach differs for a female and a male patient; what stage of disease they are going through; their financial stability because cancer treatment is expensive and even the role they play in supporting the family.

There is patient "A", a middle- aged female who has been diagnosed with an early cancer and has maximum chances of getting cured and live a good quality of life. Then there is a patient "B", a male who is the sole breadwinner of the family of two young children and a wife who has been diagnosed with an advanced cancer. "A" comes from an affluent well-to-do family while "B" doesn't have any financial backup nor any insurance.

Anybody given the option would definitely be more empathetic towards "B", but is it the right thing to do so? Think about it.

If you think from a doctor's perspective, being empathetic and subtle with "A" would help her, but for "B" it would break him down even more. The approach towards "B" if is more of giving him the courage and hope to fight the disease for all the responsibilities that he has might actually boost his confidence more and make him come to terms with the conditions better. Over-doing empathy might sometimes weaken the patient rather than doing any good and judging the right proportion of emotions is what it is all about.

❑

CHAPTER-3

The Ethical Dilemma: Balancing Compassion and Clinical Expertise

One of the most difficult decisions for an oncologist is determining the appropriate course of treatment when faced with a patient whose cancer has advanced, and curative options are limited or absent. This decision often arises in situations where the potential benefits of treatment are uncertain, and the risks and potential side effects may outweigh the potential benefits.

In such cases, we consider various factors, including the patient's overall health, their treatment preferences, the potential impact of treatment on their quality of life, and the likelihood of treatment success. These decisions require careful consideration, balancing the desire to prolong life or control the disease with the potential burden of treatment and its impact on the patient's well-being.

This decision-making process is further complicated by the fact that patients may have different perspectives, values, and priorities. Some patients may opt for aggressive treatment in the hope of gaining more time, while others may prioritize the quality of life and choose more conservative or palliative approaches.

Balancing compassion and clinical expertise is a fundamental aspect of providing high-quality care in oncology. Facing the unique challenge of merging scientific knowledge and technical skills with a deep sense of empathy and compassion for patients is not unknown to us.

Can medical intervention ever be too much? In the quest to increase patients' lifespan, does medical care negatively impact oncology patients' quality of life?

Quality of life is a descriptive term referring to one's well-being and their ability to function in ordinary day-to-day tasks. As oncologists expend energy on keeping their patients alive, it can be difficult to balance the physical aspects of cancer-related care, the psychosocial impacts of cancer, and quality of life issues that these patients face.

However, a patient-centred approach is at the core of compassionate oncology care. Clear and empathetic communication is essential and involves actively addressing emotional needs, answering questions patiently, involving them in the decision-making process and providing ongoing support throughout the journey.

It is important to note that the most difficult decision for an oncologist may vary depending on the specific case and the individual circumstances. Each patient's situation is unique, and the challenges faced by oncologists can differ from one patient to another.

Striking the balance between compassion and clinical expertise is an ongoing journey for oncologists. By prioritizing patient-centred care, effective communication, emotional support, ethical decision-making, professional growth, and self-care, we can navigate the complexities of oncology while providing compassionate and expert care to those affected by cancer.

❑

PART – II

Unmasking Cancer: Dispelling Myths and Providing Clarity

Cancer refers to a group of diseases characterized by the abnormal growth and division of cells. These cells can invade and destroy surrounding tissues and potentially spread to other parts of the body. Cancer can have multiple causes, including genetic factors, exposure to carcinogens (such as tobacco smoke, radiation, chemicals, and certain viruses), lifestyle choices (such as poor unwholesome diet, lack of physical activity and excessive alcohol consumption) and underlying medical conditions.

Several factors increase the risk of developing cancer, but having one or more risk factors does not guarantee the development of the disease. Common risk factors include age, family history of cancer, certain inherited gene mutations, exposure to carcinogens, obesity and weakened immune system.

The choice of cancer treatment depends on various factors, including the type and stage of cancer, overall health of the individual and personal preferences. Treatment options may include surgery, radiation therapy, chemotherapy, immunotherapy, targeted therapy, hormone therapy, and stem cell transplant. In many cases, a combination of treatments is used.

Advances in cancer treatments have led to increased survival rates. Many individuals continue to live fulfilling lives after completing treatment. However, cancer treatment may have physical, emotional, and social effects. Supportive care services, including rehabilitation, counselling, and survivorship programmes, help individuals manage these challenges and improve their quality of life.

Ongoing research efforts continue to enhance our understanding of cancer biology, improve diagnostic techniques, and develop innovative treatments. Clinical trials provide opportunities for patients to access cutting-edge therapies and contribute to scientific progress.

It is important to remember that each individual's experience with cancer is unique. Consulting healthcare professionals and trusted sources for personalized advice and information is crucial when dealing with cancer-related concerns.

❑

CHAPTER-4

Busting the Myths Around Cancer

Cancer is a complex and often misunderstood disease that affects millions of people worldwide. It is important to dispel myths and provide clarity about cancer to foster a better understanding. Here are some common myths about cancer and the corresponding facts to provide clarity:

Myth 1: Cancer is always a death sentence.

Fact: While cancer can be a serious and life-threatening condition, it is not always fatal. Advances in early detection, diagnosis, and treatment have significantly improved survive outcomes. Many people successfully undergo treatment, achieve remission, and live cancer-free for years.

Myth 2: Cancer is contagious.

Fact: Cancer is not contagious. It cannot be transmitted from person to person like a common cold or flu. Cancer arises from genetic mutations within the body's cells and is influenced by various factors such as genetics, lifestyle choices, and environmental exposures.

Myth 3: Cancer is solely caused by genetics.

Fact: While certain genetic mutations can increase the risk of developing certain types of cancer, most cancers are not solely caused by inherited genetics mutations. Environmental factors, such as tobacco use, unhealthy diet, lack of physical activity, exposure to carcinogens (e.g., UV radiation, asbestos), and infections (e.g., HPV, hepatitis viruses) also play significant roles in cancer development.

Myth 4: Alternative treatments alone can cure cancer.

Fact: Alternative therapies, such as herbal remedies, dietary supplements, or alternative medical practices, are not proven to cure cancer. Evidence-based treatments, such as surgery, chemotherapy, radiation therapy, and targeted therapies, have undergone rigorous testing and are the mainstay of cancer treatment. It is important to discuss any complementary or alternative treatments with healthcare professionals to ensure they are safe and do not interfere with conventional treatments.

Myth 5: Cancer is caused by stress.

Fact: Stress alone does not cause cancer. However, long-term or chronic stress may contribute to unhealthy behaviours such as smoking, excessive alcohol consumption, or poor unhealthy diet, which can increase cancer risk. Managing stress through healthy coping mechanisms, such as exercise, meditation, and social support, is important for overall well-being.

Remember, it is crucial to consult healthcare professionals for accurate information about cancer prevention, diagnosis, and treatment. They can provide personalized guidance based on your individual circumstances.

❑

CHAPTER-5

Advances in Cancer Research and Treatment: A Glimpse into the Future

Cancer treatment today involves several approaches designed to remove or destroy cancer cells and stop them from spreading.

The main treatments include:

- Surgery, which removes tumours.
- Radiation therapy, which uses high-energy rays to target and kill cancer cells.
- Chemotherapy involves drugs that attack cancer cells throughout the body.

In addition, newer treatments like immunotherapy help the body's immune system fight cancer, and targeted therapy focuses on the specific changes in cancer cells that help them grow. The choice of treatment depends on the type of cancer, its stage, and the patient's overall health, to treat the disease effectively while minimizing side effects.

The landscape of cancer research and treatment has transformed dramatically over the past few decades, moving from broad-spectrum approaches to highly targeted therapies.

As we look to the future, the momentum in cancer research continues to build, driven by innovations that promise to redefine our understanding and management of the disease.

This chapter delves into the most promising advances in cancer research and treatment, offering insights into the future directions that may soon change the face of oncology.

The Era of Personalized Medicine

One of the most significant shifts in cancer treatment has been the transition towards personalized medicine, where therapies are tailored to the genetic makeup of both the patient and the tumour. This approach has been made possible by advances in genomic sequencing, which allow for the comprehensive analysis of cancer genomes. As a result, oncologists can now identify specific mutations driving cancer growth and select treatments that directly target these genetic abnormalities.

Genomic Profiling and Targeted Therapies

Genomic profiling has already revolutionized the treatment of several cancers, including lung, breast, and colorectal cancers. As sequencing technologies become more affordable and accessible, the future will likely see routine genomic profiling for all cancer patients. This will enable even more precise targeting of cancer cells, minimizing damage to healthy tissues and reducing side effects. New targeted therapies are being developed at an unprecedented pace, with a focus on overcoming resistance mechanisms that tumours develop against existing treatments.

Pharmacogenomics

Pharmacogenomics, the study of how a person's genetic makeup affects their response to drugs—is set to play an increasingly important role in cancer treatment. By understanding the genetic factors influencing drug metabolism and toxicity, oncologists can better predict how patients will respond to specific therapies, optimizing treatment plans to maximize efficacy and minimize adverse effects.

The Revolution of Immunotherapy

Immunotherapy has emerged as a ground-breaking approach in cancer treatment, harnessing the body's immune system to recognize and destroy cancer cells. The success of immune checkpoint inhibitors and CAR-T cell therapies in treating certain cancers has spurred ongoing research into new immunotherapeutic strategies.

CAR-T cell therapy is one of the most revolutionary advancements in cancer treatment in recent years. CAR-T, which stands for Chimeric Antigen Receptor T-cell therapy, is a type of immunotherapy that involves modifying a patient's T cells (a type of white blood cell) to better recognize and attack cancer cells. This personalized approach has shown remarkable success, particularly in treating certain blood cancers like leukemia and lymphoma.

Next-Generation Immunotherapies

While immune checkpoint inhibitors have provided remarkable results in cancers like melanoma and lung cancer, not all patients respond to these treatments. Research is now focused on developing next-generation immunotherapies, including bispecific T-cell engagers (BiTEs) and immune checkpoint agonists, which may offer broader efficacy across different tumour types.

Therapeutic Cancer Vaccines

The development of therapeutic cancer vaccines represents a promising frontier in immunotherapy. Unlike preventive vaccines, these vaccines are designed to treat existing cancers by stimulating the immune system to target specific cancer antigens. Early clinical trials, particularly with mRNA-based vaccines, have shown encouraging results, and ongoing research aims to refine these vaccines for broader application.

Artificial Intelligence and Big Data in Oncology

The integration of artificial intelligence (AI) and big data into oncology is transforming the way cancer is diagnosed, treated, and monitored. AI-driven tools enable more accurate and early detection of cancer, while big data analytics are uncovering patterns and insights that were previously inaccessible.

The Promise of Liquid Biopsies

Liquid biopsies, which involve analyzing circulating tumour DNA (ctDNA) in the blood, are poised to revolutionize cancer detection and monitoring. Unlike traditional biopsies, which require invasive procedures, liquid biopsies offer a non-invasive alternative that can be performed more frequently.

Liquid biopsies have the potential to detect cancer at its earliest stages, even before symptoms appear. This early detection could significantly improve survival rates, particularly for cancers that are often diagnosed late, such as pancreatic and ovarian cancers. In addition, liquid biopsies can be used to monitor treatment response in real time, allowing for more dynamic adjustments to therapy.

Minimal Residual Disease (MRD) Detection

Detecting minimal residual disease (MRD)—the small number of cancer cells that may remain after treatment—can provide critical information about the likelihood of relapse. Advances in liquid biopsy technology are improving the sensitivity of MRD detection, which could guide the use of adjuvant therapies and reduce the risk of recurrence.

The Role of Minimally Invasive Treatments

Minimally invasive treatments are becoming increasingly common in oncology, offering patients effective options with fewer side effects and shorter recovery times. These advances are significant for patients who may not be candidates for more aggressive treatments.

Future Directions in Cancer Research

As we look towards the future, several emerging fields hold the potential to further revolutionize cancer research and treatment.

- **Synthetic Biology and Engineered Cells:** Synthetic biology involves designing and engineering biological systems for specific purposes.

  In oncology, this could mean creating engineered cells that can detect and destroy cancer cells or deliver therapeutic agents directly to tumours. This approach is still in its infancy, but it has tremendous promise for the future of cancer treatment.

- **Quantum Computing:** Quantum computing, though still in its early stages, could revolutionize our understanding of complex biological systems and accelerate drug discovery. By processing vast amounts of data more efficiently than classical computers, quantum computing could lead to the identification of new drug targets and the development of more effective treatments.

Global Health Initiatives

As cancer treatments become more advanced, ensuring access to these innovations in low-resource settings will be crucial. Global health initiatives that focus on expanding access to cutting-edge cancer therapies, improving diagnostic capabilities, and building healthcare infrastructure will play a vital role in the global fight against cancer. The future of cancer research and treatment is filled with promise. Advances in personalized medicine, immunotherapy, AI, and minimally invasive techniques are already making a significant impact on patient outcomes. As new technologies and therapies continue to emerge, the potential to transform cancer care has never been greater. By staying at the forefront of these developments, we can look forward to a future where cancer is not only more treatable but also more preventable and manageable, offering hope to patients around the world.

❑

PART – III

Beyond the Diagnosis: A Journey Through Cancer Treatment

Receiving a cancer diagnosis is a life-altering moment that sets individuals on a path filled with uncertainty, challenges, and hope. However, the journey of cancer treatment extends far beyond the initial diagnosis itself. It encompasses a multitude of experiences, emotions, and decisions that shape the lives of patients, their families, and their healthcare providers.

In the chapters ahead, we delve into and focus on the profound and multifaceted journey of cancer treatment—a journey that extends from the moment of diagnosis to the various stages of treatment, survivorship, and beyond. We explore the physical, emotional, and psychological dimensions encountered along the way, shedding light on the complexities, triumphs, and struggles faced by those impacted by cancer.

Beyond the medical aspects, we will examine the emotional rollercoaster experienced by patients and their loved ones. From the initial shock and fear to the resilience and determination that emerges, we will uncover the range of emotions, coping mechanisms, and support systems that help individuals navigate the challenging terrain of cancer treatment.

Ultimately, this section aims to provide a comprehensive understanding of the journey of cancer treatment. It serves as a guide, offering insights, perspectives, and valuable information to patients, caregivers, and healthcare providers involved in the intricate web of cancer care. By exploring the multifaceted dimensions of the treatment journey, we hope to empower and support individuals, reminding them that they are not alone or isolated in their pursuit of healing and resilience.

Let us now go beyond the diagnosis, embarking on a transformative journey that illuminates the path to hope, healing, and a brighter future for those affected by cancer.

❑

CHAPTER-6

Dealing with the Diagnosis

When individuals receive a cancer diagnosis, their reactions and responses can vary greatly depending on their personality, support system, previous experiences, and overall emotional well-being. Dealing with a cancer diagnosis is an overwhelming and life-altering experience that can leave individuals and their loved ones feeling shocked, scared, apprehensive and uncertain about the future.

Initially, many individuals experience shock and have difficulty processing the news. Some may enter a state of denial, refusing to accept the reality of the diagnosis. Individuals may feel overwhelmed by the uncertainty of their future, the impact on their loved ones, and the potential physical and emotional challenges they may face. It is normal to experience a wide range of emotions, including fear, sadness, anger, and anxiety, upon receiving a cancer diagnosis.

Acknowledge and accept these emotions, allow yourself to feel and process them. Seek support from loved ones, friends, or a mental health professional who can provide a safe space to express and understand your emotions.

Many individuals have a strong desire to understand their diagnosis and treatment options. They may actively seek out information from healthcare professionals, reliable sources, and support organizations. Gathering knowledge about their specific cancer type and treatment options can help individuals feel more in control and informed about their situation.

But when it comes to gathering knowledge, do not refer to unproven and self-made claims of people around you. Choose your environment wisely and block the noise. Seeking comfort, guidance, and empathy from loved ones, friends, or support groups can provide a sense of validation, understanding, and emotional support. Connecting with others who have had similar experiences can help individuals feel less alone in their journey.

Take one day at a time. Focus on the present moment and break down your journey into manageable steps. Set small goals, celebrate milestones, and acknowledge your resilience throughout the process. While it is essential to plan for the future, try not to dwell excessively on the uncertainties and instead focus on the tasks at hand.

It is important to remember that everyone's response to a cancer diagnosis is unique, and there is no right or wrong way to react. Be patient and compassionate with yourself as you adapt to the challenges that lie ahead. Seek support, stay informed, and draw strength from the resilience within you as you embark on your journey of healing and hope.

❑

CHAPTER - 7

Nurturing the Mind-Body Connection: Integrative Approaches to Cancer Care

Integrative approaches to cancer care involve combining conventional medical treatments with complementary and alternative therapies. These approaches recognize that a person's physical health is intimately connected to their mental, emotional, and spiritual well-being. By addressing and supporting the mind-body connection, individuals undergoing cancer treatment can experience improved quality of life, enhanced treatment outcomes, and better overall well-being.

The key components of integrative approaches to cancer care are: Food, Mind and Body. By addressing the physical, mental, emotional, and spiritual aspects of cancer care, patients can experience improved quality of life and overall well-being throughout their cancer journey.

MIND

Mindfulness practices involve paying attention to the present moment without judgment. Meditation techniques, such as focused breathing or guided imagery, can promote relaxation, reduce anxiety and stress and improve overall emotional well-being.

Engaging in counselling, support groups, or therapy can help individuals cope with the emotional challenges associated with cancer diagnosis and treatment. These resources provide a safe space for expressing emotions, reducing anxiety and depression, and developing coping strategies.

Spiritual care acknowledges the importance of addressing an individual's spiritual beliefs and practices during cancer treatment. This can involve connecting with a spiritual community, engaging in prayer or meditation, or seeking support from a spiritual counsellor. Spiritual care aims to provide comfort, meaning, and a sense of purpose during the cancer journey.

BODY

Regular exercise is beneficial for individuals undergoing cancer treatment. Integrative approaches encourage physical activity tailored to a person's abilities and preferences. Exercise can help to improve strength, reduce fatigue, enhance mood, and boost overall physical well-being. It is important to consult with healthcare providers to determine suitable exercise options.

Yoga combines gentle stretching, controlled breathing, and meditation, which can help reduce anxiety, improve sleep, increase flexibility, and enhance overall physical fitness. Exercise, tailored to an individual's abilities and preferences, can boost energy levels, improve mood and reduce fatigue during cancer treatment.

Complementary therapies such as massage therapy, acupuncture, and aromatherapy can provide relaxation, reduce pain, and improve overall well-being. These therapies can help to alleviate treatment-related side effects such as nausea, fatigue, and neuropathy and promote a sense of calm and comfort.

NUTRITION AND DIET

Integrative approaches emphasize the importance of a healthy diet to support the immune system, optimize treatment outcomes, and reduce treatment-related side effects. A healthy diet rich in fruits, vegetables, whole grains, and lean proteins can support the body's healing process and boost energy levels. Registered dietitians can provide guidance on nutrition plans tailored to an individual's needs and help manage treatment-related side effects like appetite loss, weight changes, and digestive issues.

It is important to note that integrative approaches should always be discussed with healthcare providers to ensure they align with conventional treatments and are appropriate for an individual's specific condition. The integration of complementary therapies should be done in coordination with the primary oncology team to ensure safety and effectiveness.

❑

CHAPTER-8

Dietary Care

Cancer treatments like chemotherapy and radiation do a fantastic job of killing cancer cells, but what happens when they also kill your appetite?

For treatment to be as effective as possible, patients should try their best to maintain their weight, but this is hard to do when many side effects of treatment negatively impact patients' ability and desire to eat. Fortunately, there are several strategies patients can employ to continue eating well during treatment.

Some of the common side-effects of treatment which can be managed through dietary modifications are:

- **Loss of Appetite:** It is common to not feel like eating during treatment. To counter it, prefer eating small meals frequently, rather than focusing on major meals. Munching on healthy snacks can be a reasonable option. Limiting fluid intake before and during meals is also a good way, so that you fill up on food and not on fluids. A high-calorie, high-protein intake should suffice and provide adequate nutrition.
- **Changes in Taste:** Chemotherapy and Radiation Therapy for oral cancer cases often affect the taste buds.

Marinating food before cooking or seasoning with tart fruits like lemon and lime, along with herbs and spices can be an effective way. Try sweet foods to counteract bitter, salty or acidic tastes.

- **Sensitivity to Smell:** During treatment, the very smell of certain foods can make patients sick to their stomachs. If you are plagued by sensitivity to smell, eat foods cold or at room temperature to make smells more tolerable. If the smell of food being cooked in the kitchen triggers, it is wise to keep the kitchen ventilated by keeping windows open and using exhaust fans or chimneys.
- **Nausea:** One of the most challenging side effects cancer patients face is nausea. It is important to keep weight on while in treatment, but that is challenging when the thought of eating is making you nauseated. SOS medications are mostly prescribed to counter nausea, however some diet modifications may aid as well. Juice, broth, ginger ale or other clear liquids are acceptable options to suppress nausea. When you feel like eating, choose plain foods like bread, crackers and steamed or poached fruits.
- **Dry Mouth:** Many patients struggle with dry mouth, making eating and drinking uncomfortable. To combat dry mouth, sip on water regularly throughout the day. Snack on sugar-free hard candy or ice chips. Add gravy or other sauces to food. Avoid all alcohol — even alcohol-based mouthwashes.
- **Mouth Sores:** When faced with painful mouth sores turn to liquid supplements and shakes as meal replacements. Eat soft, chopped foods like soups, mashed potatoes,

egg salad, scrambled eggs, khichdi, daliya and oatmeal. Choose cold foods over warm.

- **Diarrhea:** Drink plenty of fluids such as water, clear broths, herbal teas, or electrolyte solutions to replenish lost fluids. Avoid caffeine, alcohol, and carbonated drinks as they can worsen diarrhea. Eat small, frequent meals. Opt for mild, low-fibre foods like white rice, toast, boiled potatoes, cooked vegetables, and lean proteins such as chicken or fish. Avoid greasy or fried foods, spicy foods, raw fruits and vegetables, high-fibre grains, and dairy products as they can aggravate diarrhea.
- **Constipation:** Drink an adequate amount of water throughout the day to soften the stool and promote regular bowel movements. It is important to gradually increase fibre intake to avoid discomfort or gas. Include high-fibre foods like whole grains, oats, fruits (e.g., berries, prunes), vegetables, legumes, and seeds in your diet. Chew your food thoroughly and eat slowly to aid digestion.

Apart from these modifications, your doctor may ask you to avoid the following food during chemotherapy such as:

- Fresh fruit and vegetables, especially leafy vegetables that can hide or conceal dirt and other contaminants.
- Raw sprouts.
- Raw or undercooked meats and poultry, raw fish, salami, sausages and seafood.
- Unpasteurized beverages, such as unpasteurized fruit juices, raw milk, raw yogurt.
- Undercooked eggs, such as soft boiled, and poached.

When it comes to dietary support, it is not just about what you eat. Maintaining hygiene and food safety is equally crucial to avoid any kind of food-borne infection. Here are some ways following which can help you prevent food borne infections:

- Do not buy food stored or displayed in an unclean area.
- Do not buy bruised or damaged fruits or vegetables.
- Make sure the food that you purchase is not past its sell by or expiry date, and follow directions on proper storage.
- Rinse all fresh fruits and vegetables under running water, and dry them with a clean towel or paper towel.
- Before and after preparing food, wash your hands for 20 seconds with hot water and soap. Pay special attention to areas between fingers and under nails.
- Clean your utensils and dishes with hot water and soap.
- Disinfect your kitchen slab and cutting boards.
- If eating out, choose restaurants that are clean and that are willing to prepare your food as you order it cooked.
- Pay attention to your water source and use only filtered or RO water.
- Keep your refrigerator clean and store foods correctly at correct temperatures.
- **PRO TIP:** Maintain a food and symptoms diary. Write down or make a note of what you eat and drink and record any symptoms you experience daily.

❑

CHAPTER - 9

Regaining Body Confidence

Regaining body confidence during cancer treatment can be a challenging process, both physically and emotionally. Understand that your body may undergo changes during treatment, and it may take time for the situation to return to normal. Be patient and kind to yourself, and remember that your body is resilient.

While you may not have control over the physical changes happening in your body, you can control your mindset and how you choose to perceive yourself. It is important for cancer patients to know that there are many things that they can do to minimize these side effects.

Skin Care: Chemotherapy often causes dry, irritated skin. You can take reasonable steps before starting their treatment rather than waiting to deal with symptoms after treatment starts and then continue the regimen throughout the treatment.

- Avoid long, hot showers or baths. Hot water can cause more blood flow to the skin, which can lead to greater blood flow to areas of inflammation.
- Use gentle, fragrance-free soaps.

- Use good long-stay moisturizers to prevent skin dehydration. Creams or ointments could be preferred rather than lotions because the thicker consistency is better.
- Just be smart about sun exposure. Use a broad-brimmed hat, sun-protective clothing, and an SPF of 30 reapplied every two hours if you are outside, more if you are sweating.
- Itching is also a common problem. You may get itch relief with over-the-counter hydrocortisone creams. However, if itching interferes with sleep, oral medications prescribed by your doctor after consultation might work.
- Skin can also go through colour changes during chemotherapy, particularly with breast or colon cancer treatment. If this happens there are creams and exfoliants containing salicylic acid that can be tried.

Hair Care: Every coin has two sides. Likewise, chemotherapy treatment combats cancer cells, but unfortunately, it also leads to unwanted side effects, such as hair loss. In fact amongst the female patients, watching their hair fall out is commonly the most distressing. Hair usually begins falling out two to four weeks after you start treatment. Fortunately, hair loss from chemotherapy is temporary. You can expect to regrow your hair three to six months after your treatment ends, though your hair may temporarily be a different shade or texture.

Here are certain steps to consider to cope with hair loss:

- Opt for a wig or cap to feel more attractive.
- Hats, turbans, and scarves can also camouflage hair loss, although some people prefer to leave their heads uncovered.

- Cutting your hair short eases the inconvenience of shedding lots of hair. It can help reduce the emotional impact of watching your hair fall out.
- Perming or colouring hair during chemotherapy is a big No. You can opt for them once your treatment is over after consulting your doctor.

Make up: Wearing makeup can help you feel more confident and more like yourself when you are having treatment. However, do check with your doctor before using any skin care products.

- Colour correcting creams (CC creams) moisturize your skin and give a smooth, luminous colour to your complexion. You may prefer them if your skin tends to be dry.
- Blush can really brighten a pale, sallow or tired complexion and make your face look healthy and vibrant. Try a cream blush, which can be preferable than powder.
- Eyebrows may fall out as a result of chemotherapy. You can use an eyebrow pencil to draw out the arches and a brow filler to fill the gap.
- False eyelashes have come a long way over the years.
- Use a subtle, neutral-coloured eyeliner to accentuate your lash line and create the appearance of lashes along with a neutral palette of eye shadows.
- Chemotherapy and radiation can cause lips to flake and chap, so be sure to keep your lips well moisturized. Choose creamy, moisturizing lipsticks as opposed to matte long-lasting formulas.

Dressing: Wear clothing that makes you feel comfortable and confident. Choose fabrics that are soft and gentle on your skin, and opt for styles that flatter your body shape and make you feel good. Choose colours that complement your skin tone and draws attention.

Accessorize: Accessories like earrings, scarves, and eyeglasses can be a great alternative to shift the focal point. Choose things that not only complements your features but also draws attention and diverts one from concentrating on the pain areas.

Lastly, the most important tip. Shift your focus to your inner qualities, talents, and accomplishments rather than solely on your appearance. Repeat positive affirmations or mantras that reinforce self-love and acceptance. Affirmations can help move your mindset towards self-compassion and embracing your body as it is. Remember, regaining body confidence is a personal journey, and it may take time. Be patient with yourself and celebrate small victories along the way. Surround yourself with positivity and focus on nurturing your overall well-being throughout the process.

❑

CHAPTER - 10

Coping with Stress

Stress is a frequent companion to cancer, and it needs to be acknowledged, even accepted. People who have cancer may find the physical, emotional, and social effects of the disease to be stressful.

Factors that lead to stress in cancer patients and their caregivers:

- Worries about an uncertain future
- Managing unforeseen costs
- Problems associated with the disease and its treatment

Knowing the physical signs of stress you experience, can help one understand the causes and take action to reduce or prevent these issues.

How does psychological stress affect people who have cancer?

A cancer diagnosis affects a person's relationships, productivity, and well-being. Coping with cancer can be more challenging with added stress from work, family, or financial concerns.

Everyday stress can also make coping with a cancer diagnosis more difficult.

Stress has not been shown to cause cancer. But chronic stress may weaken the immune system, causing other health problems and decreasing feelings of well-being.

How can people who have cancer cope with psychological stress?

Emotional and social support can help patients learn to cope with psychological stress. Such support can reduce levels of depression, anxiety, and disease- and treatment-related symptoms among patients.

Tips to reduce stress:

- **Exercise regularly:** Moderate exercise such as a 30-minute walk several times a week can help lower stress. If possible, take a walk outside in a park or other natural setting. Sunlight, fresh air and the sounds of nature can help brighten a person's day.
- **Make time to socialize** with family or friends, as it is an acceptable way to lower stress.
- Maintaining a **healthy diet** and getting enough rest will give you more energy to deal with daily stressors.
- Try to **get 7 or more hours of sleep** each night. If you have difficulty sleeping, talk to your healthcare team about ways to manage sleeping problems.
- **Join a support group** as it offers you the chance to talk about your feelings and fears with others who share and understand your experiences.

- Spend time doing an **activity that you enjoy** and you find relaxing, such as reading a book, gardening, or listening to music.
- Learn a **new hobby**. Engaging in a new and challenging activity gives you a sense of accomplishment and provides a distraction from daily worries.
- Engage yourself in **relaxation techniques** such as deep breathing, meditation or yoga. These can help your mind relax and even reduce fatigue.

Some more approaches that can be helpful towards reducing stress are:

- Make a list of the things you routinely do, such as work and household chores and **prioritize** your tasks.
- **Break down tasks into smaller steps**. This process can make seemingly overwhelming problems easier to handle.
- **Be aware of your limits.** If you do not have the time, energy, or interest, it is fine to politely decline when people ask you to take on tasks. Do not feel guilty over saying no. At work, do not volunteer for projects that would make your workload unmanageable.
- **Ask for help.** It is also good sense to ask family, friends, and coworkers for help. People are likely to offer their support, so think about particular tasks you need help with beforehand.

Learn to recognize the physical signs of stress. Feeling calm and rested, prepares one to handle difficult aggravating situations with greater confidence and resolve.

❑

CHAPTER - 11

Can I Continue My Usual Activities?

While going through cancer treatments, patients often ask how will this cancer treatment affect their daily life? Those who are working, or have quite an active life worry about whether they will be able to work, exercise, and perform their usual activities? The answer is very much yes. In fact, patients always advised are not to be bedridden and stay physically active. However, one should not work to the level of getting tired or exhausted.

Usual Activities: We know it is not easy, but try to make a few changes so you do not get too exhausted. Ask your family or friends to help with chores, and have your shopping delivered if you can.

If you have to look after children, try to arrange help with childcare on chemotherapy days and for a few days afterwards. If you are looking after children, try and get them to do something relatively quiet that you can join in with or encourage from the sofa. Keep them busy without having to do too much.

With some planning and a few precautions, your social life can still go ahead. You might not always be able to do the things you take for granted. But you do not need to stop your social life completely. You may just find that you need to plan ahead a bit more.

Some tips that can help:

- Get some rest during the day if you are going out at night – you will have more energy for the evening.
- To avoid getting an infection, always eat freshly cooked food - avoid raw meat, fish, eggs, soft cheese and take away foods.
- If you have an important social event coming up, check with your doctor if the treatment schedule can be arranged in a way so that you are between treatments that week.
- Avoid family or friends who might have infections.

Work: Some people with cancer are able to continue their normal routine, including going to work, while they are still under treatment. Others find that they need more rest or just feel too sick and cannot do as much. If you can work during treatment, you might find that it helps you feel more like yourself.

Some people are able to keep working while they are getting cancer treatment. Some people work their usual full-time schedules. Some work as per the same schedules under special conditions.

However, it is important to consider the kind of job one does. If it is a stationary job one can certainly continue but in case one is required to travel to crowded places and meet several people then it should be avoided as during some phases of the treatment the patient might be immune-suppressed and this might increase their risk of catching any infection.

Exercise: In the past, people were often told by their doctor to rest and reduce their physical activity. But newer research has shown that exercise is not only safe and possible during cancer treatment, but it can improve how well you function physically and your quality of life.

Too much rest can lead to loss of body function, muscle weakness, and reduced range of motion. Regular moderate exercise has been found to have health benefits for the person with cancer. Your exercise plan should take into account any exercise programme you already follow, what you can do now, and any physical problems or limits you have.

At least 20 studies of people with breast, colorectal, prostate, and ovarian cancer have suggested that physically active cancer survivors have a lower risk of cancer recurrence and improved survival compared with those who are inactive.

There are certain conditions you need to keep in mind:

- If you exercised before treatment, you might need to exercise less than usual or at a lower intensity during treatment. The goal is to stay as active and fit as possible.
- People who were very sedentary (inactive) before cancer treatment may need to start with short, low-intensity activity, such as short slow walks.
- For older people, those with cancer that has spread to the bones or osteoporosis (bone thinning), or problems like arthritis or peripheral neuropathy (numbness in hands or feet), safety and balance are important to reduce the risk of falls and injuries. They may need a caregiver or health professional with them during exercise.

- If you experience extreme fatigue, anaemia, or a lack of muscle coordination, do not exercise.
- If you have any shortness of breath, pain, or tightness in your chest, stop exercising immediately. Discuss with your doctor to develop a plan of movements that are right for you.
- If your immune system is compromised and your white blood cell count is low (lower than 3,500), avoid public gyms, yoga studios, and other public places till your white blood cell count is at a safe level.
- If you have neuropathy or tingling in your hands or feet from chemotherapy, make sure you take care to reduce your risk of falling or injuring yourself.
- If you are getting chemotherapy to treat breast cancer that has spread to the bones, you may have a higher risk of breaking a bone. You may have to lower the intensity and duration of your workout.
- If you have undergone a surgery, you should refrain from lifting heavy weights.
- Talk to your doctor about the exercises you plan to do. You may also want to talk to a physiotherapist.

There is a famous saying by Stuart Scott that, "You beat cancer by how you live, why you live, and in the manner in which you live." So, go ahead, do your regular activities as you did earlier and be physically active. Live your life by your own terms, not cancer's.

❑

CHAPTER - 12

Caring for the Caregivers

When cancer strikes at one's door, it does not affect the individual diagnosed with it, but rather the entire family, who are the closest caregivers of the patient. While caregivers play a crucial role in supporting and assisting individuals with cancer, they often experience physical, emotional, and mental stress themselves while providing care to their loved ones.

Caregivers must prioritize their own well-being. Take breaks, rest, and engage in activities that you enjoy. Self-care is pivotal and can include exercise, meditation, hobbies, or spending time with friends and family.

Caregivers should empower themselves with appropriate knowledge to make informed decisions and reduce anxiety. Learn about the specific type of cancer your loved one has, its treatments, potential side effects, and how to manage them. Understanding the medical aspects can help you better support your loved one and communicate effectively with healthcare professionals. However, one should seek and gather knowledge from reliable sources and not just go googling everything.

Maintain open and honest communication with your loved one who has cancer. Discuss their preferences, treatment options, and any concerns or fears they may have. Clear communication can help build trust and strengthen your relationship.

While joining a support group is mostly advised to patients, caregivers should also join support groups to seek counselling and find people who share their experiences, challenges, and emotions with others as they understand their situation.

Plan your schedule. While caring for the patient is a monumental task, you cannot ignore your own jobs for that matter. Arrange for respite care from other family members, friends, or professional caregivers to get time off from your responsibilities. A duty rotation chart and time-table for each family member taking care of a particular aspect of caring for the patient can reduce the burden significantly. This allows uniform breaks to each caregiver to recharge and attend to their own needs.

Maintain a system to keep track of medical appointments, medications, test results, and important documents. This can help you stay organized and ensure nothing falls through the cracks.

Cancer treatment can be expensive, and caregivers may require guidance on financial and legal matters. Connect financial advisors or legal professionals who specialize in cancer-related issues to help navigate these challenges and manage your finances better.

Take the time to celebrate milestones, big or small, in your loved one's cancer journey. Celebrating their progress and resilience can provide a positive boost for both of you.

Remember, caregiving can be challenging, but you are making a significant difference in the life of your loved one. Take care of yourself, so that you can continue to provide the support they need.

❑

CHAPTER - 13

Life After Cancer: Preventing Recurrence

Surviving cancer is a significant achievement, but it is important to remember that the journey does not end with treatment completion. After cancer, there is a need for continued vigilance and proactive steps to prevent recurrence.

1. Follow your healthcare team's recommendations:

- Continue regular follow-up visits with your healthcare team. They will monitor your progress, perform necessary tests, and provide guidance specific to your situation. Adhere to their recommended surveillance schedules and promptly report any unusual symptoms or concerns.
- Take your treatment seriously and complete it. Care for people with cancer does not end when active treatment does. Continuing hormonal therapy is essential for individuals with hormone receptor-positive cancers. It helps prevent cancer recurrence, provides long-term disease control, improves survival outcomes, and may reduce the risk of developing new primary cancers. By

staying committed to the prescribed hormonal therapy and working closely with the healthcare team, patients can optimize their treatment outcomes and improve their overall quality of life.

2. Maintain a healthy lifestyle:

- **Balanced diet:** Focus on a diet rich in fruits, vegetables, whole grains, lean proteins, and healthy fats. Limit processed foods, red meat, sugary drinks, and excessive salt intake. A healthy diet can support overall well-being and reduce the risk of cancer recurrence.
- **Regular exercise:** Engage in regular physical activity, such as walking, jogging, swimming, or cycling. Aim for at least 150 minutes of moderate-intensity exercise or 75 minutes of vigorous exercise per week. Regular exercise helps improve physical fitness, boosts the immune system, and reduces the risk of cancer recurrence.
- **Weight management:** Maintain a healthy weight through a combination of a balanced diet and regular exercise. Obesity is linked to an increased risk of cancer recurrence in certain types of cancer.
- **Avoid tobacco and limit alcohol:** If you are a smoker, seek support to quit smoking. Avoid exposure to secondhand smoke. Limit alcohol consumption, as excessive alcohol intake is associated with an increased risk of certain cancers.

3. Manage stress and mental well-being:

- Chronic stress can negatively impact your immune system and overall health. Engage in stress management techniques like meditation, deep breathing exercises, yoga, or seeking support from therapists or support groups. Prioritize activities that bring you joy and relaxation.

4. Vaccine and screening:

- Follow recommended vaccination schedules, such as the human papillomavirus (HPV) vaccine or hepatitis B vaccine, to reduce the risk of certain cancers. Stay up to date with cancer screening guidelines, such as mammograms, Pap smears, colonoscopies, or other relevant tests, depending on your cancer history and age.

5. Environmental awareness:

- Reduce exposure to environmental toxins and carcinogens. Be aware of occupational hazards or environmental pollutants that may increase the risk of certain cancers. Take necessary precautions, such as using protective gear, maintaining proper ventilation, or avoiding exposure to harmful substances.

6. Support and community:

- Seek support from cancer survivorship programmes, support groups, or counselling services. Connecting with others who have gone through similar experiences can provide emotional support, guidance, and a sense of belonging.

- Life after cancer requires an ongoing effort to prevent recurrence and maintain overall health. By adopting a healthy lifestyle, following medical recommendations, and being proactive in self-care, you can reduce the risk of cancer recurrence and promote a fulfilling post-cancer life. Remember to stay connected with your healthcare team and embrace the support available to you on your journey to long-term survivorship.

❑

PART – IV

Finding Meaning in the Midst of Aversity: Inspiring Stories of Remission and Survivorship

Cancer is an experience that only the patients or cancer-survivors can describe with full justice who have been right where you are. We understand that no two cancer patients are alike, and neither is their treatment journey. Each patient's journey, though, has some common traits: strength, determination, persistence and sense of hope in the battle against cancer. My patients inspire me every day. On the pages that follow, I am telling their stories here, in their words, as a tribute to them.

❑

Section-I

Young Champions' Stories

Abhilasha Tiwari

| 45/F | CA Rt Breast | 2012

I was a 45-year-old housewife and a mother of two children when I encountered Cancer. It was December 2012, when I suddenly felt some itching on my right breast. I ignored and took it as a common itching but after few days it was discomforting to me. I met my gynaecologist, who examined and advised me for an FNAC and Mammography after which, I was diagnosed with breast cancer. I was shocked but later I was neutral and made myself positive because I was self-aware about the disease. I believed that this was a decision of God and if God has written it in my fate, then they will also bless me to come out from this phase.

However, I was worried about my daughter as she was in Pune for higher studies. If she got to know about my disease, she would drop her studies. So, we decided to conceal from my daughter. I discussed with my neighbour Rashmi about my diagnosis because she herself was a Breast cancer survivor. Her reaction towards me was very normal as she had also been in the same position before. She supported and guided me with everything related to cancer and suggested to me about consulting Dr. Meenu Walia.

I always wanted to visit many places, go on solo trips and to live a healthy, happy and meaningful life...After my first meeting with Dr. Meenu Walia, I felt I found the right person and my dreams would surely get true. I can never forget the encouraging words and thoughts Dr. Walia used to pass on to me and other patients. During my treatment and chemotherapy sessions I was half broken and confused but Dr. Walia used to hold my hand and say... **"Everything will be all right you will win this battle against cancer"**. Her words were my hope.

I had never gone through any hardship during my treatment, as we came prepared for the chemotherapy. We brought books and movies along with to enjoy the chemo cycles in hospital. **I never felt that I was a cancer patient.**

Only the thought of my daughter made me weak because we had still not disclosed to her about my illness. Whenever she called to ask about my day, I always tried to control my emotions and made fake stories that we were unable to talk as we were out today, etc. I felt it was harder to deal with my daughter in this situation more than the disease.

And then, finally the day came when Dr. Walia informed me that I was back on my track and did not require any further therapy and just be on follow up. **I cried along with the most satisfying smile on my face.**

We proved that 'Cancer is never the dead end'...Instead of being upset and hopeless, just take some routes from the end points of the road. Now, when I look back the whole episode looks like a bad dream and today, I am back to my normal routine life with never dying spirit, performing well in my role of good wife and mother. All I can say is, **"Always carry your own sunshine that makes your day brighter"**. Have faith in God and be positive in all hurdles of life.

I am thankful to my neighbour Rashmi, my family and relatives who supported me with their cheerful attitude. And with a warm heart I thank Dr. Meenu Walia who made the situation positive with her guidance and support and erased the name of cancer from my life.

❑

Chhaya Singh

| 31/F | CA Rt Breast | 2014

For many women, receiving the news of a pregnancy brings feelings of joy and excitement. Thoughts turn to eating well, resting and building a new nursery. I Chhaya Singh, 27 years old at that time, was also going through the same feeling.

I was 6 months pregnant, and we were expecting our first child. During my examination I discovered a lump in my breast which was not normal. I had it checked and after a biopsy was performed it was confirmed that I was diagnosed with breast cancer. I never thought a healthy and stress-free pregnancy would soon turn into a long journey of survival and recovery.

The excitement of having a new-born soon with us was overshadowed by depression. But we were hopeful, and we did not want to lose our first baby anyhow. So, we immediately moved to AIIMS but due to a long waiting time for response we moved to Dharamshila Hospital. There we met Onco Surgeon Dr. Naik and with his advice we continued my wife's pregnancy for another month and a half after which our baby girl was born.

I was apprehensive about the treatment. What good would it do for me? Would I be able to take care of my child during treatment and after that even?

One week after the birth of our baby, I underwent breast surgery and was then referred to Dr. Meenu Walia for chemotherapy. Dr. Meenu Walia explained the completed procedure of chemotherapy very patiently. I had 8 cycles of chemo and after that I was on follow-up. I tolerated the chemo easily just because of Dr. Walia's support and encouragement. I was treated so kindly and respectfully each time I came for treatment. Everything was absolutely amazing, and I felt no such side effects. I thank Dr. Meenu Walia for being a powerhouse of inspiration and encouragement for me.

Today, I am completely all right, our baby is also healthy, and we have a happy family together. Although some fear remains of recurrence, but I am focused on reasonable health and the precautions as advised by her. I am just thankful to such an amazing doctor and her team who have supported me throughout my treatment till now. I am grateful to my husband Akash Singh who stood like a rock by my side and made this journey as comfortable as it could have been.

This was our journey with cancer, and we wish nobody faces such a situation in their lives. But, if you do, then stay strong, stay hopeful and the almighty will definitely produce a miracle...

❑

Harjinder Kaur

| 44/F | CA Breast | 2016

I am a teacher at MCD School and have a happy life with my husband. My journey with breast cancer started in 2016, when I was 44 years old. I noticed a lump in my left breast while changing my clothes at home after coming back from a marriage. The lump was very suspicious and painless but in the morning it disappeared. Same moment my mind clicked about cancer so, I informed my husband about it. Without delay, we consulted a gynecologist. My doctor advised me to have an ultra-sound mammography and referred me to an oncologist. Then I met Oncologist Dr. Meenu Walia who informed me that I had breast cancer. I was devastated and stressed when I found out that I had cancer.

Suddenly I was so shocked and questioned myself, "Why Me"? Dr. Meenu Walia comforted with her words that, "Don't worry this is a curable disease". Her words motivated me to fight this disease. Dr. Meenu Walia was absolutely wonderful and after consultation, I wasn't nervous or afraid. Really, what I felt was a desire to know everything. I wanted to know my options and everything about cancer. Later I started to worry, but my first feeling was a desire to have as much information as possible about my diagnosis and treatment plan.

During treatment, I went through surgery followed by chemotherapy and radiation. As side-effects of chemotherapy, I lost my hair and breast after surgery. It was really very embarrassing for me. I developed an inferiority complex. I was afraid to go out from my home... I was affected socially and psychologically. The most difficult aspects of this time were the side effects. There were times when I wanted to give up. I was tired. There were times when I was afraid; not of dying but leaving my family.

Later I got aware about patient support groups from my doctor, where I found everybody was like me...they were all cancer survivors and enjoying their life under treatment. People at Max kept my spirits uplifted. I could not have asked for a better environment to be in. My friends there became like a second family. I got a lesson to live a new life from them. I also participated in dance performances and am happy to be part of their support group.

Today, I have recovered from the treatment and happy to report that I am back to work and have resumed my normal routines. During this very overwhelming period, it was healing to have these services under one roof. At Max, when I experienced side effects, help was always a quick phone call away. My care team responded instantly when I needed something. I never felt being on my own. My family also was incredibly supportive and never left me to fend for myself. They made sure I had a healthy diet and gave me the comfort of their homes.

I specially thank my husband who sailed through the hardship of battling cancer with me, he supported me and my children alone for everything. I also admire my group members who gave me strength with their experiences. And lastly, I never met God in real life, but in the battle of my cancer treatment I found God in my doctors who blessed me with my second life.

Looking back, I am glad that I kept my attitude positive, which helped me get through the harshest part of treatment. My faith has also helped me during this challenging time. Finally, I am thankful that Max and the entire team continues to be there for me, informing me of how to stay in good health and keeping close surveillance. Always trust your doctor, instead of information given on internet about treatment.

I learnt a lesson from life that "Ziadagi main tufaan aana bhi jaruri hai, tabhi pata chalta hai kaun hath pakad kar sath chalta hai aur kaun hath chura kar bhagta hai" *(It is necessary to have storms in life, that is when you know who will hold your hand and walk together and who will run leaving you behind.)* I realized during my cancer journey the importance of people in my life who fought along side me.

❑

Hina Siddiquee

| 32/F | CA Breast | 2009

I am Hina Siddquee, a housewife from Kashipur. I was living happily with my husband, daughter and family. Suddenly, in 2009 I found a nodule on my right breast and got concerned about it. I went to my family doctor, who suggested that I should go for a FNAC test. I was so scared when the doctor confirmed breast cancer and referred me to AIIMS Hospital Delhi. That time my mind was totally blank, and I was unable to think what would happen next. I started thinking about my end we usually associate death with cancer.

But my family and my husband gave me strength to fight cancer and we came out of our town to Delhi for treatment. We first went to AIIMS but due to a long waiting time and delay, we decided to consult the Dharamsheela Hospital. There we met

Dr. Meenu Walia. She was really like God to me as she guided me regarding my disease and its treatment. She advised for surgery as the first step of treatment which was required as soon as possible. During this phase we also consulted other doctors as we were not economically strong, but all doctors advised us to continue treatment under Dr. Meenu Walia. I found myself in the right hands with her and went for my breast surgery. During the treatment she supported and motivated me in all aspects.

Chemotherapy was really a painful time for me, and it was tough to deal with the side effects. I even lost my hair. We were also going through a financial crisis. During the treatment, along with me, my family was also affected physically, socially and economically. But with all these hurdles, I always kept my hopes high and prayed to God which helped me win this fight. My husband also helped me to stay motivated and gave me strength to beat this disease.

I admire my husband who always stayed together with me in my pains and sorrow and saw me through this journey of cancer treatment. I also appreciate Dr. Meenu Walia for her guidance which helped me to overcome all the hurdles. She is really kind-hearted and gracious in nature. Even her team was very helpful and supportive; they all helped me periodically from time to time.

I want to share my experience with others that always believe in God, don't fear the name of cancer and fight it to the fullest. Always keep yourself motivated and stay strong with the help of your will power. Now that I have overcome cancer, I perform my day-to-day chores with my children and family happily.

❑

Hunny Kapoor

| 22/M | Synovial Sarcoma | 2015

मुझमें और किस्मत में हर बार बस यही जंग रही,
मैं उसके फैसलों से तंग वो मेरे हौंसलों से दंग रही!

A Synovial Sarcoma Survivor and an Amputee aged 26 years; I am Hunny Kapoor, a Motivational Speaker, an Awardee, a Rider and a Marathoner. What differentiates us among all is how we react to situations in life. I was leading a normal teenager life, pursuing Maths (H) from DU. Being an enthusiast, I used to give home tuitions, volunteered in NGOs, working part-time in an MNC. I tried to make my own space and luck in Delhi, Panipat being my hometown.

I lost equilibrium after 4.5 years of my journey in the capital and was diagnosed with sarcomatic cancer in the right ankle in March 2015. While dating a girl, I made an appointment with doctors. My studies got affected and life turned upside down. Those were the most terrible moments of my life. Initially I wasn't able to accept the truth and hid it from my family for two days. I felt so burdened, unable to understand why it was happening to me and the troubling question "What's next?"

I cannot remember how many times I tried to end my life. But my story in God's book wasn't finished yet. Anyhow collecting my guts, I faced my parents with the situation. The tears in their eyes hit me so hard and became my strength and I consoled myself. Perhaps I could end everything with a full stop on my life, but I've no right to put my parents 22 years investment at stake. Every single moment I tried to find a reason to blame this on. Couldn't find one!

Later on, doctors suggested either I could save my life or my foot. I then made a tough choice. It took a week to convince my family to choose amputation as there was no better cure. Fortunately, I got in touch with Singapore Cancer Society and consulted them. I finally chose to fall in the category of 3 percent of Indian population. I went under a series of surgeries. Everyone anticipated I would be completely bedridden and stuck to wheelchair for life.

After my amputation, the scenario changed. My parents became more conscious of my activities. I lost all that I had gained but what I never lose is my confidence and will power. After all, a hero is not made of situations; he is the one who moulds them.

I practised walking in prosthetics and maintained the pace of my life, provided this time with more efforts. It has been 4.5 years since the amputation, I ride, commute on public transport, I swim and hit the gym daily. I'm pursuing graduation again, working in a private firm, interning as a Campus Ambassador, volunteering as a Brand Ambassador and as a business outreach with different organizations. I've been to open mic and storytelling platforms, mental health seminars, workshops for specially abled, been to events as a motivational speaker, I'm a part of the Human Library Delhi as a Human Book. I completed 20 marathons with 5 kms and 10th marathon with 10 kms. Recently, my story was shared in the form of a motivational short film crossing 4.4M → views https://www.youtube.com/watch?v=i5FOx1ub8c8. I was the core team member for Dance for Kindness New Delhi 2018 in November covering 120 cities, 50 countries with over 20,000 participants. I was fortunate enough to find a person who is aware of my story and the ups and downs, my partner. I've been awarded at different platforms and felicitated for the work I've done breaking the stereotypes being a role model.

So, cancer put a comma in my life but not a full stop. It made me a fighter and I realized who Hunny Kapoor is. At the end, I am who I am because of my family and friends. Now that I am a survivor, I meet new people with the aim to create cancer awareness and make everyone realize that if I, despite all the odds, I can do all this then what is your excuse of not doing something....?

❑

Jaya Chhonkar

| 40/F | CA Ovary | 2016

My journey of ovarian cancer started when I was suffering from a stomach infection and bloating in January 2016. I consulted my doctor and was advised for a routine ultrasound.

During the ultrasound the doctor discovered a multiple cyst and fluid in my abdomen. Subsequently they advised a CT scan. The CT scan result was the same and showed a tumor and it was diagnosed that I had ovarian cancer. The consulting doctor diagnosed as Stage III. I came to know that I had only 10 months to survive. The feeling of imminent death was really painful.

I moved to Max Hospital under the supervision of Dr. Harit and Dr. Meenu Walia. That time I was totally disheartened with the name of cancer and my first thought was "Oh my God, why have you chosen me?" As my mother had expired from the same disease and I had seen how much pain she had gone through, I was really worried about myself and my family. But by God's grace slowly and gradually while consulting my doctors, I was able to regain my mental strength and confidence.

During the treatment it was hard to bear the pain after surgery and endless nausea and vomiting during chemotherapy. My confidence was shattered, due to the pain, which was unbearable, and also worries about money.

My family, my doctor's team and my friends always stood by me in my darkest days to keep me motivated. As I am a social worker, people whom I helped earlier in their crunch times, they were praying for me and also visited my place to get me motivated. It was a surprise package for me and then I came to the conclusion that all commendable work for a social cause that everybody does, gets repaid here in this life only.

I cannot name a single person, but it was a combined effort of everyone in my life. To be specific I would thank my in-laws who took over my home so that they could take care of my children and husband. My husband always stood by me with a smile on his face, so that I could smile and be happy. My social connections prayed for me.

Last but not least, I am grateful to my doctors like Dr. Harit who was available 24 hours for me, Dr. Sanjeev, Dr. Alok and Dr. Geeta who always gave me strength to recover. Dr. Meenu Walia who helped me recover with pre-and post-chemotherapy. I am really thankful to all of them. I feel like I am reborn again for my second life.

During this battle I learned that all you have to do is be mentally strong, keep cool and calm and pray to the almighty. In my second life, I have become more humble and prepared to do my social work with great energy. I owe my life to others now.

❑

Lata Khandelwal

| 44/M | CA Ovary | 2012

I am a homemaker from Delhi. In July 2012, my world came crashing as I went to see a gynecologist with the symptoms of abdomen pain and vomiting. She advised me an ultrasound. The radiologist I consulted found a tumour in my ovary and suggested that I should get an immediate surgery. After the surgery I was asked to consult an oncologist with the biopsy of an operated tumour, as they doubted the presence of ovarian cancer.

Later I consulted Dr. Meenu Walia with the biopsy of my tumour, and she advised me for CT scan. That's when the big C word was revealed... I had Ovarian Cancer. What followed were moments of shock, numbness, cries and worries about my family. As per her guidance I went through surgery again, as she discussed the risk of reoccurrence of cancer. I was going through trauma of pain and stress as it was the question of my life, so my family members took the opinions of different doctors, but everyone suggested different treatment and it was really very painful for me to consult varied doctors after two surgeries. Later, as my conscience advised, I continued my treatment with Dr. Meenu Walia due to her positive nature and supportive attitude.

And there started my year-long journey to combat cancer between surgeries and five cycles of chemotherapy and radiation. The treatment began but what did not subside was my fears and apprehensions with the side-effects of chemotherapy. The social stigma attached with baldness and the pain of chemotherapy were something I wasn't ready to deal with. As I became bald, my social life was totally hampered, and it was very tough to overcome pain during chemo. Along with the support of Dr. Meenu Walia who guided me at every step, it was my prayers which gave me strength and kept me motivated constantly.

If there is something that drove me through was the motivation and support provided by my family. Being a part of a joint family proved to be a boon for me. My son and my sister-in-law stood beside me as strong pillars and kept me determined throughout the fight. Dr. Meenu Walia and her team guided us at each step and their support helped me immensely.

The day when I got to know about my cancer, I was shocked and started crying, worrying about my family. I left all hopes to live anymore. I believed in the myth that cancer means the end of life but today nine years have elapsed on and I am living my life as beautifully as I was before cancer. I learned cancer has a treatment and cure, if diagnosed at an early stage. All we need to do is pay attention to any abnormal symptoms no matter how trivial it is. Stay strong in your mind and soul and this will pass... Always have trust, believe your doctor and always consult a specialist. Now, even my son got married and I cherish each and every moment with my happy extended family.

❑

Malini Sharma

| 48/F | Ca Ovary | 2023

'Cancer is only going to be a chapter in your life, not the whole story'-Joe Wasser

May 9, 2023, Fortis Hospital, Gurugram

"Maliniji, aapki surgery ho gayi." As I opened my eyes, I saw faces of multiple doctors surrounding me. I regained consciousness and saw an IV stand next to me marked "Fortis Hospital-ICU 5". My first thought was, "Why am I in ICU and not in the room?" My eyes moved around everywhere, all around the cubicle. The clock showed 10 pm. I asked one of the team doctors, "Was my surgery this long?" His reply, "12.5-13 hours." Gradually, I moved my numb limbs to only know that I had an arterial catheter on my left wrist (an invasive BP measurement), two plastic drains inserted into my abdomen for abnormal fluid collection, a set of 4 intravenous IV lines on the right side of my neck (to infuse electrolytes, antibiotics and nutrition), epidural pain management system inserted in my spine, a catheter into the urinary bladder, a pulse oximeter and finally an oxygen mask. My surgeon, Dr. Rama Joshi, a renowned name in Gynae Oncology, broke the news to me that I had bad ovarian tumours, one of which had ruptured during surgery and that I had been diagnosed with ovarian cancer. Dr. Rama's voice became a distant hum, words mingling into an incomprehensible buzz. Time stood still, yet chaos erupted within. Shock, disbelief, and a numbing wave of emotions crashed over me. In that moment, it felt as if the world had shifted on its axis.

Questions raced through my mind, each one a thunderous echo, drowning the world around me. Fear gripped me, its icy fingers tracing every nerve and every thought. I couldn't believe it. Denial clawed its way into my thoughts, insisting this was a mistake, perhaps a mix-up in the test results. In the midst of the tsunami of turmoil, there was a surreal detachment, this sense of disbelief that this could not be my reality. Denial whispered seductively, urging me to reject this unwelcome news, to believe it was all a cruel mistake, a rude shock and a miserable accident in my life. My mind raced, attempting to grapple with the enormity of what I had just heard. Questions flooded my mind, unanswered and daunting. What does this mean for my future? How severe is it? Do my loved ones know? Anger flared within, a surge of frustration at the unfairness of it all. ***Why me?*** What wrong did I do? It felt like an injustice bestowed on me by the almighty, a cruel twist of fate! Emotions tangled together—sadness, frustration, and an overwhelming sense of vulnerability. Tears welled up, an involuntary response to the overwhelming flood of emotions that threatened to consume me.

I requested to see my attendants. My son was first to come in. I held his hand. My tears and the silence between us explained all the unexplained! Being fond of cars and holding back his tears, he whispered, *"Gaddi kharab ho gayi hai, theek ho jayegi!"* My husband was next to come in, looking tired, perplexed as if, together, we had both lost the battle and surrendered to the unreasonableness of destiny. At 12 am IST, I passed on the message to my attendants waiting outside, to wish my daughter (who was studying at LSE, London) a very "Happy Birthday" from her mother. Thereafter, I was administered sedation and the air in the room grew heavy, suffocating almost, and then every sound seemed to fade into an eerie silence as I closed my eyes into deep sleep.

The next morning, I enquired about being shifted to the room. The staff assured me that this would certainly be done by late evening. I saw my son and my husband again during ICU visiting hours at 11 am. Looking at their stressed faces, my unwillingness to worry them more, in the heart of this relentless storm, I portrayed an unyielding resilience, painting hope in our hearts amidst the daunting landscape of cancer.

As Dr. Rama Joshi explained the prognosis during her daily rounds, outlining the treatment plan and offering untiring support, her words came as a lifeline amidst the storm. In the midst of the devastating news, there emerged a glimmer of hope-a belief that amidst the darkness of the fearful diagnosis, there might still be a path towards healing and towards a future reclaimed!

Malini Sharma

Dear readers, my name is Dr. Malini Sharma. I was then a 48-year-old cancer warrior and now a cancer survivor. By profession, I am an Associate Professor in the Department of Economics at Daulat Ram College, University of Delhi. We are a family of four—me, my spouse, our son and daughter. We stay in Noida. In my life, I have always strived to be a perfectionist—perfect husband, perfect home, more than perfect children and a perfect job embodied with an impeccably flawless work-life-balance. Fitness wasn't just a routine for me but a lifestyle that I had effortlessly woven into my days, complemented by a firm dedication to enjoying life's pleasures. Adventurous by nature, I was always willing to accept new challenges, whether it was conquering a mountain trail, hang-gliding, scuba diving, travelling or diving headfirst into spontaneous escapades. Boredom, for me, was a foreign concept. Being always well dressed, abreast with the latest fashion and make-up, according to all our friends, always so prim and proper. Beyond my physical prowess, also lay a heart brimming with joy and contagious love for life lived king size! Fit as a fiddle, high in spirits and super proud of my strength and vigour, I considered myself to be in everlasting best of health and overall well-being. I detested doctor appointments, regular check-ups due to my false belief that I was never going to fall sick. Ironically, my late father being a doctor, my fear of doctors, fear of pain and anxiety about medical procedures was overwhelming.

My journey with ovarian cancer began in April 2023, when after a bout of irregular periods, commonly observed as symptomatic of menopause, I had excessive bleeding for approximately 25 days and my gynaecologist prescribed an ultrasound. Initially we cracked jokes on ***"MEN-O- PAUSE",*** but to our shock, the ultrasound led to an MRI, a CT scan and back to an ultrasound. The diagnosis was ovarian cysts (eventually, malignant tumours), a suspicious biomass below the right ovary with intermediate risk of malignancy, pelvic endometriosis and the presence of fluid in the fallopian tubes, often referred to as hydrosalpinx. The recommendation was surgery in a multi-speciality hospital. We were still optimistic and thought that the tumour would be benign, as I had no visible symptoms and CA-125 test and other tumour marker tests were negative for malignancy. Then came the grind to find a suitable doctor. My brother-in-law's friend headed the blood bank in Fortis, Gurugram and Dr. Rama Joshi was highly recommended by her as having performed more than 500 plus such surgeries. During my long and harrowing surgery, the frozen section tested positive for malignancy and one of the tumours ruptured too. Thus, post-surgery, I was diagnosed with ovarian cancer, stage II.

The moment of receiving a cancer diagnosis is incredibly challenging, carved clear in memory and can evoke a complex mixture of emotions. There is an initial shock, emotional turmoil, physical weakness and the faint spark of resilience that might arise deep within, during this pivotal moment in a cancer patient's life. Believe me, my dear readers, it is this ***"spark"*** that we have to keep alive for the rest of the treatment.

As days went by in the hospital, while walking amidst the quiet whispers of the hospital's ward corridor, watching other patients probably in a worse condition than mine, I found the strength to embark on a battle I never expected. As Dr. Joshi's team of doctors Dr. Rashmi, Dr. Tarini, Dr. Manas, Dr. Mishra and

Dr. Rama Joshi herself, came to see me twice a day, answered all my queries patiently, and made me as comfortable as they could, although the diagnosis still echoed in my mind. However, now with a newfound courage that stirred within me, ready to face the unseen adversary. As we looked forward to discharge after 9 days, knowing that I would have to undergo adjuvant chemotherapy, my husband told me numerous times, that there was no option but to fight. Every time, I looked at him, I visualised stepping into the ring, armed like a soldier with courage and unwavering determination to face this formidable challenge of life.

June 6, 2023, Max Hospital, Patparganj, New Delhi

My first session of chemotherapy was with admission at Max Patparganj for insertion of the PICC Line. There was my first meeting with my medical oncologist, Dr. Meenu Walia. She happened to be friends with my surgeon Dr. Rama Joshi and without wasting time, unresistingly, she called Dr. Joshi and they communicated about me in a manner that was comforting. Chemotherapy was a gruelling experience, not just physically but emotionally and mentally as well, but something that I needed to come to terms with.

June 13, 2023 onward, Max, Noida

Each weekly session of chemotherapy was a plunge into an uncertain abyss, where the promise of healing intertwined with the harsh reality of side effects. The anticipation before each treatment was a mixture of hope and dread—a battle waged in the heart, where courage clashed with the fear of the unknown. The sterile walls of the treatment room bore witness to the tumultuous emotions that surged within. The scent of disinfectants mingled with the bittersweet aroma of hope and anxiety. As the IV, dripped life-saving drugs into my weary veins, it felt like a paradoxical infusion-hope mingled with the poison that aimed to eradicate the disease.

Loose motions, pain following Grafeel injections, fatigue, mouth ulcers, skin peels, rashes, hair loss, cramps and the metallic taste lingering in the mouth became constant companions, reminders of the battleground within. Each day brought a new war against the relentless assault on the body, a struggle to find solace in moments of discomfort. The mirror reflected not just physical changes but also the emotional scars, a stark reminder of the toll taken by the treatment. On 31st July, Dr. Walia started targeted therapy alongside chemotherapy. This was a smooth transition, all thanks to Dr. Meenu Walia's expertise.

Amidst the physical distress, emotions ran like a turbulent river--days of despair were eclipsed by flickers of optimism induced incredibly well, by Dr. Meenu Walia and her team of doctors, notably, Dr. Maneesha. There were moments of vulnerability, tears shed in solitude, and silent screams against the unfairness of it all. Yet, within the depths of despair, glimmers of resilience emerged—small victories celebrated with doctors and nursing staff at Max, Noida, amidst the overwhelming challenges. Being the only child of my parents, and one of the most loved daughters-in-law of my in-laws, my birthdays had always been celebrated in special ways. One of my chemotherapy sessions was on my birthday and I was in an awful mood. Even though, I did not tell anyone of my birthday, but knowing my DOB from my documents, Dr. Meenu Walia ordered a chocolate cake for me. This personal touch by a doctor like her touched my heart and filled me with immeasurable gratitude and believe me, this was one of the best birthdays of my life celebrated with all the other patients like myself, doctors and all nursing staff at Max.

The support of loved ones—my husband, our children, my in-laws, my mother, friends, neighbours and relatives, their reassuring presence, their prayers and unwavering encouragement were like rays of sunlight breaking through ominous clouds. Their love became a lifeline and a source of strength when the weight of treatment threatened to overwhelm.

My husband has been the strongest pillar of support for me. His words, "Babes, this too shall pass", miraculously lifted my moods. Every time I held his hand, I felt warmth and immense solace. He has been a true companion in these trying tumultuous times which had not only taken a huge toll on me, but also on him as he went along with the treatment without leaving me alone and without any respite for himself, at the cost of his business, social and personal life. My daughter continuously reminded and motivated me that there is a ***"can"*** hidden in the word cancer. My mother-in-law used to spend time with me between chemotherapy sessions, always filled me with so much positivity. My father-in-law, at his age, walked to the mall and bought silk scarves for me. My mother prayed for me every single day. My brother-in-law facilitated my treatment by introducing us to both Dr. Rama Joshi and Dr. Meenu Walia. I am truly blessed to have great family support. In the midst of this tumultuous journey, looking at the faces of my near and dear ones, and the hard work of my doctors—a quiet courage blossomed—a courage, born not just from the will to survive, but from the strength to endure. Each session became a testament to the unswerving spirit, a relentless pursuit of life beyond the confines of illness. And amidst the chaos of treatments, a flicker of hope remained--a beacon guiding through the darkest of nights, a belief in the possibility of a future free from the shadows of cancer.

Through the valleys of despair and peaks of resilience, emerged a survivor—not merely marked by the struggle, but adorned with unparalleled bravery. My survivorship was not merely a status, rather it was a badge earned through endurance, courage, and an unshakable spirit. It was a testament to the power of the human will, a triumph that spoke volumes about the undefeatable strength of the human soul. It is the result of efforts and constant diligence of one's doctors—our lifelines!

My Message

To, my fellow warriors,

I know the road you tread feels daunting, marked by uncertainties and challenges that seem insurmountable. I have walked that path, felt the weight of the diagnosis, and faced the fears that come with it. But amidst the darkness, there is a resilience within you that is waiting to be unleashed, of which you are also not aware as yet. Cancer may have invaded our lives, but it can never define our spirit. We are not just victims—we are warriors in a battle, fighting with courage that knows no bounds. The journey is arduous, marked by moments of anguish, but also by unexpected successes. In the depths of treatment, I found strength I never knew I possessed. It wasn't just about enduring surgery or chemotherapy sessions; it was about summoning the nerve to face each day with hope. It was about finding beauty in the smallest victories-a smile, a moment of peace, a surge of resilience that whispered, 'I can do this'.

Ignite your passions. We have only one life—live it like never before. Do whatever makes you happy, something that you always wanted to do like painting, writing, designing and so on. Practise positive affirmations, such as saying to oneself that, "I am healthy, I am fine". Gratitude and spirituality also help in this journey. Chant God's name whenever and as much as you can. Be grateful to God almighty for being in the hands of the best doctor, such as Dr. Meenu Walia, grateful to have caring nursing staff, grateful for family support, gratitude for every morning that you see, every morsel of food that you are able to eat, for every molecule of air that you breathe.

Yes, there were tears—moments of despair when the weight of the battle seemed unbearable. Crying is not bad at all. It is a great vent out, so cry when you want to. But within those tears, do bring out a silent resolve an unspoken promise to yourself that you wouldn't let cancer steal your joy or define your future. Through the support of loved ones, the compassionate care and technical expertise of medical professionals such as Dr. Meenu Walia, and the unshakeable spirit within, I discovered an unspoken truth, "we are stronger than this disease". Our scars are not just marks of pain, they are medals awarded for our courage, reminders of battles fought and won every single day. Embrace the moments of joy, celebrate the victories, and cling to hope even in the darkest of hours. Your resilience is a beacon of light, illuminating a path for others who walk this journey. Think about the day in your life, not too far way, when you will be able to inspire others!

To every woman in the throes of this fight, I want you to know that you are not alone. Your journey is uniquely yours, but there is a community of warriors who stand beside you offering support, understanding, and steadfast solidarity. I request every lady to take out time from your daily chores and prioritise your health. Never take stress about anything—work stress, stress on family relations, stress about children, stress about differences with your spouse, etc. Remember, you can never please everyone at the same time. Therefore, give yourself utmost importance and go for regular check-ups, ultrasounds, mammography, wherever required. In case of an unexpected diagnosis such as cancer, please do not delay in treatment.

Lastly, please have faith in your doctor and her medical team. I often used to say to Dr. Meenu Walia, that, "you are the best doctor in this field and I trust whatever treatment you plan is in my best interest." She has always been a patient listener, despite the huge rush in her OPD. Never leaving any stone unturned in answering all queries, managing each and every side effect and above all, giving the best treatment protocols. Currently, post the 6 cycles of chemotherapy, I am undergoing targeted therapy for a minimum of 1-2 years, as per her advice and I am extremely happy with the treatment that has ultimately perhaps, made me *cancer-free*.

She is an excellent oncologist with an expert medical team (especially, Dr. Maneesha) with specialized knowledge in treating cancer. Trusting her expertise is reassurance enough, that you are in capable hands. I am short of words to express my gratitude for Dr. Meenu's exceptional care and unwavering support throughout my journey. Her dedication to my well-being has been an incredible source of strength during a challenging time. Her compassion and commitment to guiding me through each step of my treatment have been nothing short of remarkable.

Being a doctor as well as professor too, her ability to blend medical knowledge with genuine care has not only aided my physical recovery but has also eased my emotional burdens. I have been lucky to have been in the best hands, Dr. Meenu Walia and Dr. Rama Joshi. Their dedication to their profession, their knowledge, treatment protocols and compassion towards patients is truly commendable, and I am profoundly grateful for everything they have done for me. Whilst, I/we may face the cancer battle, only once in a lifetime but these resilient warrior doctors are fighting such battles with every patient every single day. We may come and go but they remain eternally deployed in this battlefield.

With all my love, strength and positivity,

A fellow warrior-survivor

❑

Manju Khullar

| 45/F | CA Left Breast | 2013

I got to know that I had breast cancer on October 26, 2013 at Aditya Birla Hospital Pune, but something was wrong with my body from 2011 onwards as I touched 40…

I felt a lump in my left underarm...some changes in my breast as it turned hard ...giving a feeling of fullness as one experiences during feeding… I underwent mammography but nothing was clear. Deep inside me I had this feeling that I had cancer, but reports were not clearly indicating. It became clear in October 2013.

On November 4, 2013 I got mastectomy done for the left breast followed by chemotherapy and radiation. My chemo and radiation were done under the supervision of Dr. Advani in Mumbai and Pune. After a gap of two years, I was again diagnosed with cancer in the bones in the lower back. Again, I went through chemotherapy and radiation under the guidance of Dr. Shona Nag in Pune but this time the doctor advised me for a longer treatment of five years. My treatment is called hormonal therapy or targeted therapy with the miracle medicine herceptin and perjeta. This treatment started at Jehangir Hospital Pune and subsequently at Max Hospital Patparganj and Vaishali under the guidance of Dr. Meenu Walia. All this happened as I shifted from Pune to Delhi.

When I got diagnosed with cancer...I asked God, Why me? l had beautiful hair which I lost twice ...my looks changed...had put on excessive weight...but never lost hope... All credit goes to my husband...my best friend...

Special thanks to Dr. Meenu Walia with whom I felt I was in safe hands. She is a very good doctor and an excellent human being.

My life is still the same as during the last 10 years. I have not lost my routine. l take good care of my husband, my son and my lovely house and of my plants. l don't regret cancer....it has made me a better version of myself. More humble, more forgiving... l appreciate life, every day, every second. l thank God for giving me the opportunity to meet some wonderful doctors and staff of hospitals in Pune and Delhi....

❑

Manju Yadav

| 27/M | CA Rectum

I am Manju Yadav from Bijnour, I am a home maker. In 2012 after my delivery, I felt pain in my abdomen and rectum for a month which I ignored but later I also started observing blood in my stool. I consulted my gynecologist in my town. She advised me Colonoscopy. She found a few nodes in my rectum and referred me to a surgeon for surgery. The surgeon examined and referred me to Dharamshila Hospital in Delhi. That time I was really afraid, and my mind was filled with questions like what had happened to me and why had my doctor referred me to a cancer hospital.

We came to Dharamshila where I was advised to go for Biopsy and CT scan in which I was diagnosed with rectum cancer.

I was totally shocked and started crying that why God gave me cancer. I had just got married 2 years ago and had recently given birth to my daughter. I felt my life had stopped and was near its end. But with the support and guidance of Dr. Meenu Walia I went through chemotherapy and radiation as a treatment and later went through surgery and my rectum was removed.

It was a really tough time for me to take care of my 3-month old daughter, as I was shifted to Delhi for treatment. We went through mental, physical and financial trauma. It was very painful while going through chemotherapy, I lost my hair, and my social life was totally over. It was very tough for my family members to manage things. My family members especially my husband helped me to overcome this battle. He always kept me positive towards my treatment and also motivated me from time to time. It was really his efforts which made things possible for me during the fight against cancer. My belief in God and my prayers blessed me with cure and a second life.

I was very fortunate to be treated by Dr. Meenu Walia. She is very positive and supportive in nature and with her guidance I got motivated to fight my cancer and become a survivor soon. Her whole staff helped me during this journey.

Now I happily lead my life with my family and daughter who has started going to school and addresses me as 'mamma'.

❑

Mudit Kumar Khatana

| 35/M | Astrocytoma | 2017

I Mudit Kumar Khatana, 36 years old, born in the family of a farmer at village Hasanpur Kalan, district Meerut, Uttar Pradesh and educated till class 12 in a Hindi medium school near my village, further qualified for the state level engineering examination, completed Bachelor's degree in engineering from state government engineering college, qualified national level exam and joined BHEL (A Maharatna Status Organization) for official career. I am tilted towards social welfare activities village level.

I would like to share my experience since last more than 1.5 year, which is as follows first six months I was having the feelings of twitching left side of face, arm, leg and numbness/heaviness occurrence in these areas, other symptoms include mood or personality changes, speech problems or blurred vision, changes in ability to think and learn etc. and was taking very lightly, even though I visited a cardiologist and physician and gone through related diagnosis, but everything was perfect. Further I had already planned for kidney stone (size of 2.5 cm) treatment in upper calyx of kidney on March 5, 2018 and went through Percutaneous Nephro lithotomy (PCNL) surgery at Fortis Hospital, Noida, after few days the frequency of the above listed symptoms increased on a daily basis. Then I discussed the same with my urologist during follow ups after kidney stone surgery dated April 20, 2017, he suggested to visit Neurologist, in the same hospital, I visited the neuro physician and explained the symptoms and went through diagnosis (like MRI, blood tests, ECG, Colour Doppler, etc.) as per doctor's suggestion. These diagnoses reports declared that I had brain tumour in the left temporal lobe of my brain dated April, 21, 2017 (Evening). I lost my confidence and became emotional, but at that point of time, this was as coincidence that my father was with me, he told one thing at that moment "Don't worry, nothing is impossible nowadays".

I visited many famous neuro physicians and surgeons, all suggested that surgery is the right and first step to start treatment and after surgery tumour blocks will go for biopsy and based on the report further treatment will be decided. I decided and went through surgery on April 25, 2018 by Dr. Anil Kumar Singh, Neurosurgeon and Director, Max Institute of Neuroscience of Max Multi Specialty Hospital, Dehradun. I was feeling well and good after surgery and was discharged within 3 days, i.e., May 28, 2018 and tumour blocks were sent by hospital for Biopsy. After the biopsy report, the tumour type was declared "diffuse astrocytoma WHO Grade-II" for that neurosurgeon referred me for Chemotherapy and Radiotherapy. For the same I had a consultation with Dr. Meenu Walia, Director, Medical Oncology, Max Multi Specialty Hospital, Patparganj, New Delhi for chemotherapy and had a consultation with Dr. Sandeep Agarwal, Head of Radiation Oncology Department of Max Multi Specialty Hospital, Vaishali, Ghaziabad. The required diagnosis took place as suggested by the doctors. In radiotherapy 28 sittings took place and in chemotherapy 12 cycles took place, treatment ended at on June 13, 2018. During chemotherapy I want to share a few things, in the beginning when I started my chemotherapy 6 cycles were recommended and when I was at 6th cycle then new recommendation came for young patient of 12 cycle in place of 6 cycle, hence doctor recommended me for further 6 cycle, also during my chemotherapy, I never had fever, lose hair, lose weight (even weight increased) and never found myself under "No appetite ascendant", otherwise during chemotherapy patients don't like to eat food and lose their weight and hair fall as well. I am very thankful to my Neurologist, Radiation and Chemotherapy Oncologist during my treatment.

During the whole treatment, I got full and fantastic support from doctors, friends, my office, society as well as family members specially my wife, by which I never lose my positive thinking and confidence. With that I got promotion at my official organization and set me as a role model for example to fight such kind of hurdles and to achieve each and every goal.

❑

Rajni Kant Ranjan

| 36/M | Embryonal Cell Carcinoma | 2012

There was nothing 'good' about the morning that day. It was the day when I came to know that was very close to death. Like any other person, I switched on my computer and started doing my research on the best cancer hospitals and doctors who could get me out of this nightmare. I found out about Dr. Meenu and somehow felt that she was the only one who could help me fight this battle.

My parents advised me to go to Mumbai, but I was automatically drawn towards Delhi. When I first met Dr. Meenu, I was very frightened, but she asked me why I was so worried. I had an outburst of emotions as I started crying profusely in front of her. She then consoled me and told me that everyone has to go one day but if I had faith in God and myself, I would be fine in a few days.

She started my treatment on November 2, 2012 and on November 23, 2013, I was completely cured. Ever since then, I have been regularly consulting Dr. Meenu and truly, she has been my saviour. Some decisions indeed change your life. Mine changed when I decided to trust my life with Max.

Cancer taught me never let fear stop you...

❑

Rishabh Malan

| 23/M | Osteosarcoma | 2013

I was 22 years old when I was diagnosed with Osteosarcoma in February 2013. I was healthy and had no symptoms. I was a B-tech student, and my studies were prolonged for 2 years after diagnosis of cancer and during the course of treatment.

"I think the key to handling cancer is to stay strong and continue your life. You have to take cancer in your left hand and throw it behind you, go forward with your right hand and stay physically active".

It was not easy for me to accept the diagnosis. My family was shattered with bad news. It was a difficult phase of my life.

My treatment plan was drawn by Dr. Meenu Walia. Chemotherapy was very painful and it has side-effects. Due to the side effects I dropped my B-tech course for years.

Even though coping with a cancer diagnosis can be difficult, I was able to move through it somewhat stoically, in part because I was prepared. That has always been the way in my family: Let us pull our socks up and carry on.

Max Super Specialty Hospital, Patparganj played a huge role in providing hope and support. The hospital was comfortable, which made all the difference. And after just a short time there, everyone on the staff felt like family. Every time I turned a corner, someone gave me a hug. It meant so much to my family too. They drew comfort from the fact I received such wonderful care. My family was also an incredible support system.

My family was always with me during those tough times. It was their motivation and belief which provided me strength to beat this fight of cancer. I used to read many books on cancer survivors by renowned authors which not only kept me motivated but gave me a new perspective towards life. My family and my eldest sister were my pillars of strength during that tough time. Also, I would especially like to mention the priceless contribution of Dr. Meenu Walia in my treatment who gave me a second life.

Recovering from cancer is a powerful experience. It is very difficult to explain, but there is newness in life. I'm seeing and hearing things differently. It has been an exciting time too to think about the future. My key learning during the journey of cancer was that, take life as it comes, never be afraid of the outcome, give your best shot. Just live in the present and be prepared for the future. Also, at the end I would like to quote a phrase which is very real and holds true in every sense. "God helps only those who help themselves".

Now, my life is changed again. After I completed treatment in 2013, I had joined my engineering college again. I had completed my B tech in July 2016. Also I go to the gym daily, and do workouts for 1.5 hours. I got placement in one of top private company, and I am also looking for government jobs for which I have joined a coaching institute. More than ever, going through this experience has made me realize that every day is a gift.

❑

Sonia Bansal

| 37/F | Ca Breast | 2021

I once basked in the radiance of a blissful life alongside my loving husband, daughter Saanchi, my mother, and my brother-in-law Ankit and his wife Rachna. Our days were filled with boundless happiness and simplicity, till the forces of fate intervened, forever altering the course of our lives. At the tender age of 37, God had a different plan in store for me.

It all began with a routine visit to my gynaecologist to address a concerning lump in my body. While the doctor dismissed it as a regular occurrence, an unyielding intuition compelled me to insist on an ultrasound. Little did I know that this seemingly innocuous decision would set us on a tumultuous path we never could have anticipated. When the ultrasound results arrived, the doctors chose not to discuss them with me directly, instead calling my husband Amit. The weight of our fear became an oppressive force that enveloped us. Amit was summoned into the doctor's cabin, where the chilling words were spoken: "She is suspected to have cancer. We need to conduct a biopsy and a CT-Scan." Our world crumbled in an instant, and though the pain was profound, we resolved to conceal our worries till the final report arrived. On that fateful day, December 23, 2021, the dreaded news was confirmed: breast cancer.

Our once serene family dynamic had been irrevocably shattered. Shock and disbelief permeated every corner of our lives. We had led modest lives, finding solace in the simple joys of home-cooked meals, rarely indulging in dining out. Drinking and socializing were alien concepts to us. Amit, shouldering the weight of demanding work commitments, seldom found respite from his professional end eavours. Our careers had soared to great heights—I, having recently been promoted to Vice President, and Amit transforming his company into a thriving organization with 350 employees. Just weeks before the diagnosis, we had joyously celebrated my brother-in-law's first anniversary.

In the midst of this whirlwind of despair, Amit sought solace and guidance from his cousin, Pawan bhaiya, a beacon of wisdom and inspiration. Together, they embarked on a journey to meet renowned oncologists in Delhi/NCR, seeking counsel from experts in the field. After countless discussions and emotional turmoil, we made the resolute decision to embark on the arduous path of treatment under the exceptional care of Dr. Meenu Walia, a reputed medical oncologist at Max Patparganj.

Tears streamed down our faces when we first met Dr. Meenu Walia. My young daughter, Saanchi, at the tender age of 7, struggled to comprehend the gravity of the situation. Further investigations revealed that I was battling stage 3 cancer, requiring chemotherapy, breast surgery, and radiotherapy.

Throughout the harrowing journey of battling cancer, I confronted countless traumatic experiences that etched indelible imprints on my spirit. One of the most emotionally challenging aspects was the loss of my hair and eyebrows during chemotherapy. Witnessing strands of hair fall relentlessly and gazing at my reflection in the mirror, devoid of my familiar features, served as a constant reminder of the fierce battle raging within me. It felt as though a part of my identity had been cruelly stripped away, intensifying the emotional torment that gripped me from within.

Chemotherapy, with its potent drugs, unleashed a torrent of side effects that ravaged my body. Waves of nausea crashed over me, robbing me of respite from sickness. Fatigue consumed me to the very core, sapping every ounce of energy I once possessed. Anxiety, fuelled by the fear of the unknown, gripped me tightly, amplifying the already overwhelming emotional toll of the treatment. The relentless pain coursing through my body served as a constant reminder of the havoc cancer was wreaking within me.

Finally, the seemingly interminable cycle of chemotherapy came to an end, and Dr. Gita advised that I proceed with a breast removal surgery on May 21, 2021. This marked yet another traumatic chapter in my journey. The physical agony I endured was excruciating, but the emotional scars ran far deeper. The loss of a part of my body, a symbol of femininity and womanhood, left me feeling vulnerable and shattered. Each glance in the mirror became a painful reminder of what had been taken away, magnifying the grief and testing the depths of my resilience. We were utterly broken, and though our family sought to portray strength, I could sense the silent tears shed behind closed doors. Each stage brought forth its own set of pain, and the journey of recovery was prolonged due to persistent issues with the surgical stitches. It took nearly six months for my wounds to heal, thanks to the unwavering steadfast support and extraordinary efforts of Dr. Gita and the entire team led by Dr. Abhishek.

Just two weeks after the surgery, Dr. Rashi prescribed 20 sessions of radiotherapy. The treatment left my skin blistered and seared, pushing me to the very brink of endurance. Radiotherapy, yet another critical phase of my treatment, brought its own share of pain and trauma. The sessions were gruelling, and the beams of radiation left my skin burned and blistered. The anguish I endured during this process was beyond imagination, and amidst the searing pain, finding solace proved to be an arduous task.

Once the gruelling radiotherapy was completed, Dr. Meenu advised me to undergo 14 sessions of maintenance therapy, a scaled-down version of chemotherapy aimed at preventing a relapse.

In the midst of my battle, Saanchi matured far beyond her years, shouldering responsibilities and blossoming into an independent young girl. Amit selflessly shouldered the burden of my care, taking charge of our daughter's needs, from getting her ready for school to managing countless other tasks. Ankit, Amit's younger brother, stepped up and assumed responsibilities that were once Amit's, while Rachna and my mother ensured that I received the utmost care, from providing nutritious meals to offering unwavering support. My in-laws stood resolutely beside us throughout this challenging period. Pawan bhaiya and Charu bhabhi emerged as our saviours, extending their helping hands whenever we needed them.

For those devastating 18 months, we chose to keep the details of my struggle confined to immediate family and a select few trusted individuals. Amit made this decision to shield us from unnecessary distractions, enabling us to focus solely on my recovery. He temporarily put his business aspirations on hold, revealing the truth to only a handful of key personnel within his organization. Despite my insistence that he concentrate on his work, Amit emphatically declared that businesses could be rebuilt, but the bonds with loved ones were irreplaceable. My fervent wish is that no one in this world should ever have to endure the wrath of this insidious disease.

The emotions we experienced throughout this journey ran deep, carving indelible marks upon our souls. It was a road filled with anguish and torment, yet our resilience held firm. Through the unyielding love and unwavering support of our family, we found the strength to face each hurdle head-on. Cancer may have wreaked havoc upon our lives, but it did not define us. Our story is one of immeasurable fortitude, boundless love, and an unyielding determination to emerge victorious against all odds.

Throughout this arduous journey, I faced countless hospital admissions, totalling 25-26 times. There were moments when I struggled to breathe, prompting midnight rushes to the hospital, intensifying the profound sense of fear and vulnerability. Amidst this turmoil, I am grateful that we had the means to afford the necessary treatments. The financial burden could have shattered us completely, but we were fortunate enough to have the resources to navigate through this difficult period. Cancer had dealt us a cruel hand, subjecting us to unimaginable pain and trauma. But amidst the darkness, there were glimmers of light—moments of unwavering support from loved ones and the unyielding strength that emerged from deep within. Our family rallied together, shouldering responsibilities, providing the care and love I needed to navigate the depths of this disease.

During the last 18 months, I continued to work and received great support from my mentor Deepak and the entire team. The support that I got from my team members was truly incredible, and it filled my heart with gratitude and a sense of belonging. Their unwavering encouragement and empathy touched me deeply, providing a ray of light in the midst of my battle with cancer. Their constant presence and understanding made me feel valued and supported, instilling in me a renewed sense of hope and determination.

I ensured that work kept me busy and occupied, not only to stay productive but also to distract myself from the hardships I faced. The team's camaraderie and collaboration became a source of strength for me, giving me the courage to face each day with resilience. Their kindness and compassion made me realize that I was not alone in this fight, and together we could overcome any obstacle.

During this journey, one of the driving forces that kept me motivated to fight my battle with cancer was none other than my precious 8-year-old daughter, Saanchi and my mother as there is no one to look after her if something happens to me. The immense love and inspiration I found in Saanchi's innocent eyes fuelled a fierce determination within me. I refused to let cancer confine me to the corners of my home, instead actively participating in every activity I could. I vividly recall a Holi event organized by Meenu Ma'am and the team, where my name was not initially included for a stage performance. But I was adamant. I wanted to be a part of it, to soak in the joyous atmosphere and embrace every moment of life's vibrant colours. I didn't want to dwell in the shadows, cursing my fate. Instead, I chose to immerse myself in the activities, living each minute with an overflowing spirit of joy and gratitude.

Reflecting upon this journey, I am reminded of the fragility and resilience of the human spirit. Each trial and tribulation has left its mark on me, but I refuse to let cancer define me. Instead, I choose to embrace the unwavering fortitude, boundless love, and unyielding determination that carried us through the darkest moments. Together, we have faced the unimaginable, emerging as a testament to the power of resilience and the strength of the human spirit. We stand strong, united, and ready to conquer whatever challenges lie ahead.

❑

Tanisha Gaurav

| 37/F | CML | 2014

"My name is Tanisha Gaurav, and I am a patient of CML. In 2013, I was admitted to hospital for my second delivery. After four days, I had a hard cough, and the doctor advised a complete blood work. In my test results, Total Leukocyte Count (TLC) was highly elevated and the doctor suspected blood cancer.

My world came crashing. I was in denial. I was not ready to accept how a simple cold can be related to cancer. I repeated my tests in a different lab and the results came back the same.

After the confirmation of my diagnosis of CML, I was totally emotionally drained. I held my 9 days-old new-born child in my arms and was clueless about my future. I was extremely worried about my family. My son was so unfortunate not to have been nursed by me, and helpless I cried the whole day. I felt I had lost life and had only a few days to live.

A hopeless me, dragged my body into the chambers of Dr. Meenu Walia whom my treating doctor had advised me to consult. Right from the first consultation she had given me a fresh lease of life and guidance and worthwhile counselling. She made me believe that CML is a curable cancer and there is nothing to worry. She advised me routine medications, relevant investigations and proper follow up.

After the moment I came out of the consultation, I was determined to fight. I had to win over cancer for my son. I had to come out as a warrior for my family. I had to be strong and be their strength.

I had full faith that I would make it at any cost and started treatment. I consider myself fortunate that I got immense support from my husband, my family and my doctor who stood by me like rocks and helped me sail through this battle against blood cancer.

From the age of 9 days to 9 years today, both my son and I have stood the test of time and feel blessed to be able to continue with motherhood. I am really thankful to the almighty God, my family and my treating team for my rebirth."

❑

Vaibhav Singhal

| 36/M | Germ Cell Tumour Left Testis | 2012

On January 22, 2012, I had a urine infection for which I went to a practising urologist Dr. Shekhar Vajpayee in Agra who was treating my kidney disease for the last 18 years. Here, I would like to tell you that year in 1995, my kidney was removed due to multiple kidney stones that led to malfunction when I was just 17 years old and at that time 11 major operations were done in 8 months due to my kidney stone related disease.

When I went to Dr. Shekhar Vajpai, he himself checked me on the ultrasound machine and there was a possibility of any lump or tumour in my body, then he did some tests and colour ultrasound, and it was clear that I had grade 2 testicular tumour. So, he did an operation on January 25, 2012 and removed the tumour, testis and the tubes related to it and sent them for a biopsy. When the report came 10 days later, it was confirmed to be cancerous.

When the news was broken to my family, the whole family was very nervous, but I remained courageous, and I explained to my family there is no reason to panic. Cancer is not an incurable disease in today's time and its treatment is possible. On the same day I left for Tata Memorial Hospital in Mumbai with wife.

After going there, I submitted my reports to them for review and they also confirmed cancer. I asked them to start treatment but due to an excessive rush in the Tata Hospital, I was given a date after 30 days to start treatment. When I came to know about the delay in initiating the treatment, I then understood the whole process of treatment from them and got my case transferred to Delhi and came back from there because I did not want to delay my treatment.

So, on the 18th of February, I left Mumbai for Gwalior and after reaching my home on the 20th, I left for Delhi on the 22nd and on the advice of my acquaintance there, I contacted Dr. Meenu Walia at Dharmashila Cancer Hospital. After she saw my case, she prescribed the same process of treatment as meationed to me at Tata Hospital in Mumbai.

After taking my and my family's consent, when they did some tests like PET-CT done, it showed that a new tumour had started to develop at a new place in my body, so without wasting time, Dr. Meenu Walia began to treat me through chemotherapy on February 25, 2012. I started with four cycles of advanced chemotherapy in five consecutive months post which I was brought into safe mode.

There have been many ups and downs in my life in these five months. Sometimes my hemoglobin reduced, sometimes platelets and sometimes a severe infection, but I, my wife and Dr. Meenu Walia did not give up and after five months of continuous treatment, I was re-examined through PET-CT. Dr. Walia told me that I was now in safe mode and the symptoms of the disease had completely gone from my body, but for the next few months and years I would have to be under their observation. I started going to her and got my check-up done every month.

This process went on for about 1 year, then I was called at a gap of three months, in the meantime, Dr. Meenu Walia left Dharmashila Hospital and started serving at Max Hospital Patparganj. Since then, I get all my tests done at Max Hospital at an interval of every 3 months. Today I am fully satisfied with my disease and Dr. Meenu Walia's treatment.

To tell you about myself, I never cried during my entire treatment, nor did I ever lose my courage and did not let my family cry. Whenever I was near my mother, wife and children, I always kept laughing. I had taken it as a challenge that I have to defeat cancer at any cost. I had full faith in myself and my supreme Lord Bholenath that nothing would happen to me.

All this while during the difficult times, my wife and mother supported me in my fight against this disease day and night and they did not let me break down. And I did not let them break down.

Today, when I have completely come out of and conquered my disease, I realized that we should not be afraid of this illness, rather we should face it with courage and not let our morale break because during the stay in the hospital, I felt that more than half the people do not win this disease just because they get scared by the name of this disease and lose their morale.

In that case, the hard work and medicines of the doctor also become ineffective on the patient. In this context, I always remember a line that…"रुक जाना नहीं तू कहीं हार के कांटों पर चल कर मिलेंगे साये बहार के…" (Don't stop feeling defeated… you will encounter blooms after defeating the thorns…)

I pray to my Lord that he never gives this terrible disease to even an enemy…

After I came out leaving this disease behind, I felt that I had become very weak and now I will hardly be able to do any work, but I rested for about 2 months, and revived my full courage and passion. After taking the name of Lord Shiva, my deity, I got back to work.

I started giving time to my work and family to the best of my ability and started working harder and more diligently than before. The result is that I am doing my business in a much better condition than before I got sick. I am also running a cowshed which cures sick and accidental cows. I am serving as the Joint Secretary in the famous Shri Achaleshwar Mahadev Temple in Gwalior and am fulfilling all my social duties with full responsibility.

Today, when I find a cancer patient, I tell him the same thing, do not give up and have full faith in your doctor and your God, then like me, you will definitely win this battle of cancer.

❑

Vani Verma

| 31/F | CA Breast | 2019

It all started in October 2019, when I unknowingly felt a lump in my right breast and alerted my husband, Piyush Bajaj, about it. I was 31 years of age. We immediately met with a gynaecologist, not knowing that a breast surgeon would have been the best to consult in this scenario. After the first round of mammography and FNAC, the lump was diagnosed as benign. And to our relief, we only thought of excising it before leaving the country. We were planning to move out of India in a few months and parallelly preparing for the same. After meeting a general surgeon, Dr. Pradeep K Misra, who agreed on lumpectomy, we went ahead with the surgery at Sant Paramanand Hospital in Civil Lines, Delhi. I was particularly scared because never before did I have a surgery. It went smoothly and didn't pain as much as I had expected. When the excised lump was sent for biopsy, the report suggested that it was in fact malignant! I was carrying Invasive Papillary Carcinoma grade 3 with triple negative receptors. This worried my doctor and he suggested that I should go ahead with a completion surgery under a Breast Oncologist. The outbreak of this news was so sudden and shattering. Here I was, who had left her job, planning for a future outside my country with my husband, receiving a least-expected-life-changing news. As much as it was difficult for me and my family to accept it, we were under a financial strain as well. Both, my husband and I were out of our corporate health insurance and understood that we had to bear the medical expenses on our own. Of course, we had our family's support but now, we were prepared to break our savings for our future and start with the treatment.

On Dr. Misra's advice, I came to Max Hospital, Vaishali, and met Dr. Geeta Kadyaprath. She is an expert in this field. Along with being a fine breast surgery oncologist, she is a great human being. She counselled me and my family at length and explained the further course of my treatment. We were not only apprehensive, but also clueless about why to go ahead with another surgery, followed by Chemotherapy and Radiotherapy? She patiently answered all our questions. She not only made sense but also empowered us at every step. I remember her telling me, "An alive person is flexible. Rigidity is a sign of death. You have a situation at hand, and you have two choices—either be flexible and accept the changes in your life and adapt to them or sit back and do not do anything about it. I would suggest that you be flexible and give life a chance." Those 30 minutes of conversation with her made me and my family confident to go ahead with the suggested treatment.

I had my PET scan, whose report was encouraging. It did not show any spread of the cancer, but I still had a long way to go. My paternal grandmother and paternal aunt had cancer in their lives. They had not survived the disease. My mother in particular was really worried about it.

I underwent breast conservation surgery which was completion lumpectomy and lymph node biopsy with Dr. Geeta. Thankfully, the biopsy also suggested that there was no further spread of the malignancy. This time the surgery and the days after were very painful! My wound wasn't healing as speedily, as expected. But the day we had planned for another stitch and staple, it had healed miraculously. It relieved both my doctor and me.

Immediately after my surgery, I had started with Ovum stimulation as well. I am a young woman and wanted to plan a family with my husband in the coming year. But the onset of cancer and its treatment apparently had an impact on my fertility. Dr. Geeta and Dr. Sowjanya explained it to me and suggested mature oocyte cryopreservation. Initially, it was all Greek to me, but they helped me understand that it was a procedure to preserve my oocytes, which might help in facilitating pregnancy in future. It was a tough call for me and my husband, as we had not expected anything like this. But with his support and that of my family, I went ahead with the procedure. It took me 10 days, numerous injections and a minor surgery to preserve the oocytes.

A week later, I met my Medical Oncologist, Dr. Meenu Walia. She is a very calm, composed, and brilliant doctor. She also heard me patiently and suggested the course of treatment. Till now I was still not sure as to why I was undergoing chemotherapy, because I was tumour free and there was clinical sign of cancer in my body. She, however, explained to me that since I had a family history, and got this disease at a young age, it was all the more important for me to undergo chemotherapy, which was adjuvant or preventive in nature. She also suggested that I get my hair cut short or get myself a wig.

I got my hair chopped, and to Dr. Meenu's delight, I looked pretty good! My treatment began, and I had a dose-dense chemotherapy, which lasted for about 5 months. Four fortnightly cycles, and 12 weekly cycles. The chemotherapy was tough. Its known side effects are real! It not only makes you physically weak, but also has a psychological impact. Hair is a woman's pride. Losing it is dreadful. When I got my head tonsured after my second cycle. I cried for one full day. My skin and nails also worsened.

I had decided to embrace myself and my situation, as it is. I decided not to cover my head and let everyone around me accept me the way I am. Yes, it is painful even for your family and friends to look at you like that. But what the hell! We have to win this fight together. I went for all my sessions in the best of spirits. I used to dress as for my office, took my bag, sunglasses, and the mask to go for every session. I even posted my stories on Instagram to break the stigma around someone having cancer or being treated for it. I had realised that cancer is a not a death sentence. It is not something we have invited or should be punished for. It is a disease, and we should fight it just as we fight the other ailments. Back home, we had a great environment. We had set the countdown and celebrated every single session completion. My nephew used to come and dance with me each evening. All the positivity and prayers enthused my will to survive the treatment.

The outbreak of Covid-19 had scared us all. We were not sure about how to visit the hospital or how safe would the premises and the staff be and whether or not we should expose ourselves to the infection. My immunity was suppressed due to chemotherapy. My husband, who accompanied me to the hospital was exposing himself along with me. But we had a reassuring experience at Max Hospital. They took the utmost care of ensuring that cancer patients, like myself are kept safest. The dedicated Cancer Day Care facility was well guarded. It was sanitized every 30 minutes. I am also grateful for their nursing staff. They are not only well-trained, but also well kept. They are a happy lot, who always greet you with a smile. My chemotherapy sessions were indeed cheerful.

The radiotherapy was conducted under Dr. Dinesh Singh. He is a gentleman with a clear mind. It took me 19 sessions for completing it. The whole treatment, from the first surgery to the last radiation, it took us about 8 months and completed in July 2020. Eight long months, during which we saw a complete lockdown due to Covid-19 as well. I have seen the anxiety on my doctor's faces, when even they were scared for immune-compromised patients like us. The frontline workers who were at the risk of the disease and exposing it to the others. It was an insane time!

My journey till now has taught me the value of gratitude. Today, I am more grateful for every conversation I have with my family, I am grateful for the silent and strong support of my life partner, I am grateful for a healthy body, I am grateful for every happy meal we cook and share. Never did I feel so loved and wanted in my life before. My husband didn't miss a single visit to the doctor with me. He stood by me patiently in all my chemotherapy and radiotherapy sessions. I didn't realise it then, but in hindsight, and retrospect. I can imagine how difficult the treatment is even on the caregivers and our near and dear ones. This disease has taught me how to live and live well.

❑

SECTION - II

Midlife Ninjas Stories

Indu Yadav

| 52/F | CA Breast | 2019

In August 2019 I saw my nipple retracted and I talked about this to my daughter. The very next day she took me to the gynae and there she advised me to do a mammography first. My mammography report came showing BIRADS 5 which meant that there was 95 percent chance that I had breast cancer. The doctor advised me to go to a breast specialist and she referred me to Dr. Geeta Kadyaprath. She did my biopsy and it showed that I had cancer in both breasts. I had bilateral breast carcinoma...stage 2a in my right breast and 2b in left breast.

My husband got tense and my daughter started crying but I remained calm and prepared myself for this new journey which life threw at me...I was not at all worried and kept smiling. My first thought was to remain calm and to make myself ready for further procedures because it is particularly important to keep our will power strong to fight against any disease… it is not only about cancer but about any problem.

It took around 9 months to complete my whole treatment which included surgery, chemo sessions and radiation therapy. I began my chemo under Dr. Meenu Walia. Although I always felt tired after every chemo session, my chemo sessions went very well and were very good. My experience with chemotherapy was acceptable because of my diet…I didn't lose weight, but I gained that however, my radiation was somehow painful. Radiation therapy didn't let me eat; my skin burned very badly. That time I thought why this happened to me...only! Surgery took my breasts; chemo gave me baldness and weakness and radiation burned my skin. It is not easy to see your body with so many things happening. You feel like giving up, but you must keep yourself strong even if you are not feeling anything.

Throughout this journey I had my family with me...my husband, daughter, son and my whole extended family were there with me. They never keep me alone. At all times I had someone with me in my room. Not for a second did they leave me alone, so I literally didn't get any time to think about problems. I was just enjoying my self…we made fun of my different looks…and cancer brought me closer to my family members. Alone it is not possible to handle physical and mental pressure...they used to share inspirational stories of survivors with me. My daughter took charge of being my caretaker and used to give me small portions of healthy meals at different times. She literally did everything beyond her limits. She used to stay awake late at night till I slept…she used to come with me early in the morning to my chemo sessions...she kept all her ears and eyes on me…all the time... Even if I felt an ulcer was popping up on my tongue, she fed me with ice-cream. She gave treats to me after every chemo session; healthy treats; home-made dishes...She even celebrated my completion of treatment.

Next came my doctors and the staff at the hospital. They provided me with easy solutions for every problem of mine. Onco Day Care doctors and staff were so pleasant...they never got irritated by our number of questions and confusions...doctors were available 24*7 for us. Whenever I faced issues with my health after chemo...I just texted them or called them and they replied within an hour. Doctors and staff made my journey easier at the hospital.

Before I never thought about travelling much...but now after battling cancer, I want to live my life at the fullest...I want to travel...because life is very short you never know what life will throw at you next...so live every single second of your life. Before I never gave importance to my health but now, I started motivating my family members to get their tests done or to female members to never conceal health issues with your family members. Today, I felt more confident leaving the shy me behind.

Cancer taught me that we should always remain positive in every situation...and should enjoy every moment of life...we should not get worried...because if there is a will there is a way... In case of my journey, I learned if you want to live life...even if you have a life-threatening disease you need to keep your will power strong that I will resolve to surely pass through this time...

❑

Kamaljit Singh Parmar

| 56/M | Non-Hodgkin's Lymphoma | 2013

I was a contractor before my disease.

In 2013 I was suffering from tonsils for a long time, later I was started with temperature also. I took advice from my family doctor, he suggested a CBC test. In the report he found my leukemia counts were so high and later he also advised me for FNAC and biopsy of my nodule as he was in doubt of cancer. By results I was diagnosed with NHL cancer which was Non –Hodgkin lymphoma.

As I got to know that I was diagnosed with cancer my doctor advised me to consult an oncologist. I visited Dharamshila and consulted Dr. Meenu Walia. With her guidance and treatment, she blessed me with a second life to live longer. When I met her the first-time during my appointment, I was so afraid and demoralized with the myths of cancer. She guided and motivated me reassuring me that my cancer was treatable. As per her guidance, I went through chemotherapy for six months which was very painful and unbearable. I was unable to take my proper diet as I was suffering with nodes in my throat, I was usually on fluids for long.

Due to the chemotherapy side-effects, I was rushed to the emergency many times but with the support of my family members specially my wife who always worried about me and stood by my side during the whole treatment. And my doctor who always guided and supported me with her encouraging treatment I have overcome the battle of cancer. During my treatment my belief in God increased and I started praying for my cure and good health.

Now, I not only lead a healthy life but also run my own restaurant.

❑

Krishan Chander

| 51/M | NHL | 2009

On one of the regular days, I noticed a swelling around my right ear, but I ignored it assuming that it was nothing major. Later on, when the swelling increased, my colleagues suggested that I should consult a doctor. Post check-up I was diagnosed with cancer in April 2009 at stage IV. I was more than frightened. and started thinking about my future as to who would take care of my wife and two daughters.

I knocked on Dharamshila Hospital's door during this obstacle of my life. There I met Dr. Meenu Walia who handled my case. I underwent 8 chemotherapies and during that process, I was also diagnosed with bone marrow cancer. This was indeed a very difficult time for me and my family. But I had faith in God and Dr. Meenu Walia, who had been treating me for so long. I continued to fight this hardship with the help of my family only to emerge as a winner. I defeated cancer in 6 months. They say that if you are positive about something, you can overcome any difficulty in your life.

After she was transferred to Max Hospital Patparganj, I also shifted there as I had only one thing on my mind that I would be under her treatment only. I thank her from the bottom of my heart for what she has done for me and my family. She has literally fed life into a corpse or else I would have died 12 years ago.

The Oncology Department of Max Healthcare not only provided me with excellent treatment but great counselling as well. They brought in hope and encouragement to my life. Dr. Meenu provided me with constant support and the Day Care Staff was affectionate and friendly as well. It is not easy to treat an untreatable disease, but Dr. Walia made it possible. She not only cured me but has also treated many of my associates whom I had referred to her successfully.

Today, my life is shining bright, all over again. As they say, the greater your storm, the brighter your rainbow. I have lived the true meaning of this sentence in my life, literally!

❑

Manju Katyal

| 55/F | CA Lt Breast | 2014

Life is as beautiful as flowers; happiness is its colours, fragrance but just like autumn life fades when disease hits this happiness. This was the exact feeling that drenched me in January 2014, when I encountered a sharp pain in my left breast and a cyst inside. I went for a routine examination at Max Hospital. I was examined by Dr. Geeta who then suggested that I should undergo a biopsy, which confirmed that I had breast cancer. Tears never left my eyes for days, but then I asked myself was I so feeble? Wasn't I capable of overcoming this hurdle?

Everyone motivated me through the entire process to make me overcome this fear and encouraged me to undergo surgery and further treatment. I underwent surgery on February 2, 2014 and I strongly believe that I was reborn that day. After my successful surgery, I was referred to the most experienced and remarkable Dr. Meenu Walia for medical oncology and chemotherapy. Jittery and still weak, I was surrounded by many prejudices about chemo. I gathered a lot of information about chemotherapy via books and internet, which demotivated me to the care. It was a nightmare of sleepless nights, immense physical and mental trauma.

I was scared when I went for my first chemo sitting with Dr. Meenu; but her pleasant smile calmed my nerves. She explained the entire process and gave me the confidence to face this challenge like a warrior and showed me how pleasant life can be after this battle is over. I lost almost all my hair, but I accepted my new look with humility and patience, the entire staff use to tell me "mataji all is well" and in full Bollywood glory I used to say to my belongings "All is well". All went well; indeed, I used to feel suffocated in entering that radiation room but hats off to the medical personnel and staff who handled my case with utmost patience and modesty. This really helped me in going through my radiation sittings and I successfully completed this part of the treatment as well. I never dreamt of stepping on a ramp to do a walk, but Max gave me a platform to fulfil this fantasy.

Dr Meenu Walia always assisted me with her care and support which helps me lead a life with so much positivity. Max champion group is my family, which loves us, supports us and cares for us to the core. This Max family is my world, and I am proud to be a member of this beautiful world.

❑

Meenakshi Malhotra

| 56/F | CA Ovary | 2014

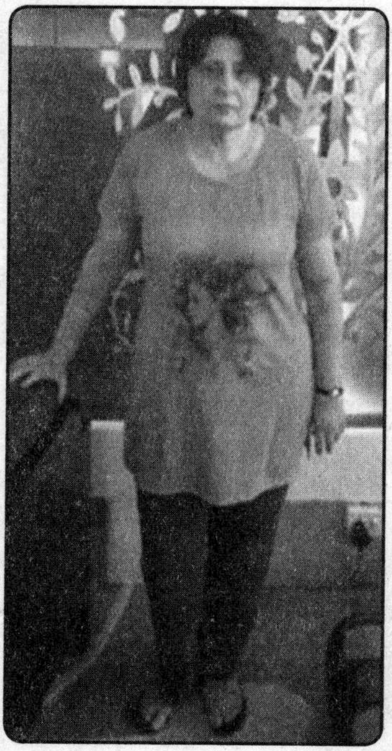

Yes, I am alive. After suffering from that, dreaded disease “cancer” I am alive... The journey has been tough but...with the support of my dear husband, daughter, family, my will power, my doctors, and most importantly God I could sail through smoothly from that situation. It seems smooth but it was tough, very tough indeed. Gathering myself every day was a big challenge that I had to encounter with myself.

I overheard my husband and sister talking about my illness... Lying in my bed, I couldn’t at first believe my ears. When both of them realized that I was not actually sleeping, they got a little conscious but then I only consoled them and assured them that I was not scared. I was rather positive that I would be abosutely fine and I think that this faith of mine in God has really helped me come out of it. My doctors, specially Dr.Harit Chaturvedi and Dr. Meenu Walia have contributed immensely in helping me to fight this disease.

When I retrospect, I find those days to be very long and never ending. Every week going for the chemotheraphy was taxing, piercing of needles either for blood investigations or chemo would give me jitters and when the nurse asked me once, if it pained, my answer was..... blank, no reaction actually...did not really know how to react but told her that at times I feel like crying and sometimes laugh aloud... confused...

I've always heard people saying 'God Why, Me'. But I Challenged Him and Said.... God ...try me.

The time has passed....slowly but as they say, slow and steady wins the race and I have come afar.... right to the finishing point which for me is the "Starting" one.

❑

Meeta Roy

| 58/F | CA Breast | 2017

I am Meeta Roy and I was a teacher by profession. It was November 2017 when I felt a lump in my breast. I immediately took the decision and came to Max Hospital and met Dr. Meenu Walia who planned my treatment without any delay.

She referred me to Dr. Geeta who did my surgery in December 2017. In January 2018 I was again back under Dr. Walia for chemotherapy. I went through 16 sittings of chemo followed by 11 sittings of radiation therapy. By September 2018, my treatment was over and since then I come for a regular follow-up.

When we got to know that I was suffering from breast cancer, my daughter and other family members panicked. They were extremely worried but on the contrary, I was chilled out. I remember I asked Dr. Walia about which stage of cancer was I suffering from and remained calm throughout. She told me that it was Stage IIb.

However, it was during chemo when I faced some difficulties. Accepting myself without hair was tough. I used to wear bandanas to style myself. I lost my appetite. But my doctor was my biggest source of motivation. My daughter, son-in-law, sisters and specially my nephew kept my morale high. Family support is really important. They all took great care of me. The staff at the hospital also were very supportive, especially Azaad, Jessy and the sisters of day care. I am very pleased with the treatment that I got at Max Hospital; my doctors gave me immense power to fight this disease.

All this while I never thought of giving up. I would also tell anyone who is battling cancer to be brave and courageous. Have confidence and everything will go smoothly. Personally, I have become bolder, stronger and more confident post cancer. So, have faith and face the challenge fearlessly.

❑

Narinder Kaur

| 57/F | Plasmacytoma | 2011

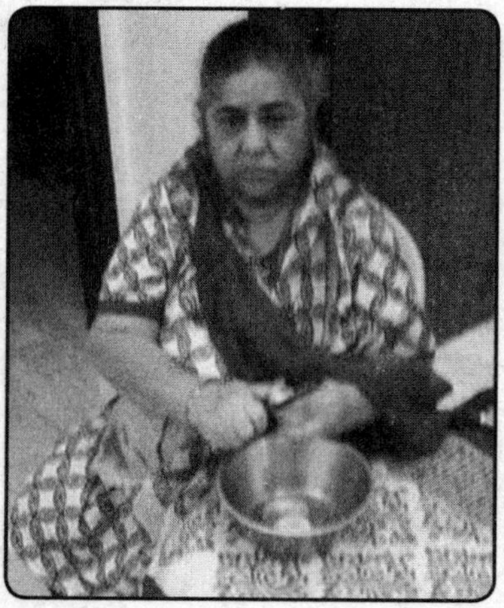

In May 2011, I was diagnosed with cancer in my neck bone. I was very disheartened when I got to know about the disease, as cancer is a word that scares everyone. Then I met Dr. Meenu Walia who started my treatment. She is a very positive and inspiring person. She reduced my pain and sorrow which I was going through. I went for a few radio therapies which were part of my treatment.

My family and Dr. Meenu Walia played a very important role in my getting well and coming out from this disease.

It has been 10 years now and I am perfectly all right. From time to time I go for regular check-ups as prescribed. Now I want to inspire all those who are suffering from cancer with my story.

Just remember that cancer doesn't control your happiness or your life. You should have the will power to fight with this disease. You should not give up and stay positive in life, as it is not the end of the world.

I have been treated very well by Dr. Meenu Walia. My doctor says hope is the bridge that will connect cancer and recovery. I now lead a very healthy, happy and normal life. May God bless all the patients suffering from this disease and help them to come out of it.

❑

Praveen Gupta

| 59/F | CA Rt Breast | 2010

I am Praveen Gupta a homemaker. My journey with breast cancer started in February 2010. In February 2010, I noticed severe rashes on my body and consulted a skin specialist. I went through 20 days of treatment, but the condition was the same. After that the gynaecologist referred me to a surgeon in Dharamshila Hospital and after a certain test I was diagnosed with breast cancer.

As part of the treatment, I was advised to remove my breast and also initiate Chemotherapy and Radiotherapy. Later, I was advised for hormonal therapy for 5 years.

When I came to know about breast cancer, it was like the end of the road for me. It was the feeling of imminent death. But with support of my family members and doctors, who encouraged me to fight with cancer, I got my mental strength again and I wanted to live again for my family.

Cancer was the toughest phase in my life. It was very painful during chemotherapy. I was down with side-effects but still my will power and support of Dr. Meenu Walia always gave me strength to cope and recover. She really taught me that tough times don't last forever.

My concern for family and the future of my children was always the reason behind my motivation. I devotionally prayed to God to cure me soon. My family supported me very well. They always stood by my side, especially my husband who helped me sail me throughout this fight. Dr. Meenu Walia always guided me positively for everything, which I needed for my treatment.

I learned from this journey of my cancer treatment that one should always be positive and motivated and be mentally prepared for treatment. Now, I am leading a healthy life.

❑

Pushpa Jha

| 55/F | CA Breast | 2018

It was in October 2017 that I felt some abnormality in my left breast. I observed a black spot on my nipple which caused no trouble/ discomfort. Initially I ignored it and did not mention it to anyone. There was no change visibly in the next six months. In early April 2018, I mentioned it to a young lady, my next-door neighbour and a close confidant. She insisted that I should consult a doctor without losing any time. A senior gynaecologist in LBS Hospital and a friend advised me to consult Dr. Geeta Kadyaprath at Max PPG. An appointment was fixed, and I visited her on April 9, 2018. She advised certain investigations/tests including biopsy of both breasts and the worst fear was confirmed. She referred me to Dr. Meenu Walia the same day.

I was diagnosed with invasive ductal carcinoma grade 2. After PET scan, there was another shock for me. My cancer was metastasized. The news was so shocking that I trembled with fear, the fear of the unknown. The world had come to and near and dear ones. They all came into my thought. I thought that my journey of life would soon come to an abrupt end.

My treatment started from April 19, 2018, with weekly chemotherapy. However, after four cycles of chemotherapy, the whole-body PET CT scan (16.7.18) showed significant response to therapy which was really encouraging and a morale-booster for me. After completion of 6 cycles of chemo (24.8.2018) three weekly maintenance doses was started. The PET-CT scan of March 4, 2019 gave me immease relief. The doctor told me that my cancer had gone to complete remission. The maintenance doses are still continuing.

My normal life was entirely disrupted. Besides traumatic experience during treatment at the hospital, even home was no different. Living a secluded life, I had to cope with side effects of chemotherapy, along with many dietary restrictions. My body did not appear to be my own. What to talk of day, it was difficult to spead an hour. I became a mental wreck and was emotionally shattered, living life on a day-to-day basis. Nevertheless, my inner strength and courage was the only source of inspiration in the given situation.

Initially, I had given up. But soon I realized that I had to complete a few unfinished tasks. I mustered all my courage and decided to fight it out. My young unmarried daughter, who refused to join the PhD. programme in a US university to look after me, gave me a cause to overcome the disease. Though shattered himself my husband stood like a rock behind me. He reminded me of a quotation of His Highness the Dalai Lama that "when you are faced with a difficult situation, don't ask why me, say try me.' I was quick to understand that this is like any other disease and I have to fight it out.

I started my day with a prayer and determination to make it great and better than yesterday. I led a regulated life with daily exercise, yoga, pranayama, regular puja and above all strict regimentation as advised by the doctor. At times, I used to slip depression. To get over this I started reading books on positivity like "The Secret" by Carnegie, "I am a Survivor' by Dr. Vijay Anand Reddy and religious scriptures. My association with Buddhism and the support of the group members was of great help to overcome pessimism. I am still continuing with all these and many more practices like chanting, healing, etc.

It is very difficult to name one person. Other than my immediate family, friends and neighbours, if I have to single out one person, that is a young lady, Smita, my next-door neighbour who substituted for my daughter when she went abroad for higher studies after my recovery. Smita has been a big moral support to me since the beginning. She was the person who fixed my first appointment with the doctor at Max. She has been a friend, philosopher and guide to me. She visits me on a regular basis, talks to me and reassures me that I have defeated the disease.

At the hospital, let me start with the leader of the team—Dr. Meenu Walia. Besides being a renowned physician, she is an excellent human being. When you visit her for consultations she first comforts you. In the beginning itself, she told me that she would do her best provided I cooperated and followed all her instructions in letter and spirit. Ma'am is a good leader. Every member of the team is not only cooperative but courteous too. On visiting Onco day care staff members first smilingly welcome you and treat you as if you are part of a family, excellent teamwork, ma'am.

Last, but not the least, my sincere thanks and gratitude to one and all who stood by me in this testing time, especially my daughter, sister and my husband, wonderful doctor and the support staff at Max Healthcare Patparganj, Delhi. My special gratitude to Dr. Meenu Walia who gave me the hope of survival in my darkest hour.

This disease has brought a sea change in my attitude towards life. A worrisome person, full of negativity, complaining type that I used to be, now I am a completely transformed person. Having no expectations, today I am more positive and spiritual than before. I extend my helping hands to others and share my happiness with them. Each day is a gift of God. We should express gratitude for everything that we have and live life fully.

Life is precious and fear is its worst enemy. Even in an adverse situation one should remain positive and optimistic. Cancer is not death. It is merely a passing phase. Besides family support, which is very important, I feel that patients should understand the responsibility of handling the situation themselves. They should follow the doctor's advice diligently, take care of their nutrition, maintain good hygiene and fight with a positive attitude. Above all, one should urgently consult a doctor on observing any kind of abnormality in the body.

❑

Ruchi Dhawan

| 46/F | Metastatic CA Breast | 2014

I, being the only child of my parents got the undivided love and attention and grew up to be more independent and able to fend for myself better, as my parents didn't spoil me by tending to my each and every need. An Indian family with a daughter as the only child was also rare in those times. But they never made me feel it and I could never ever think that being a girl I need to restrict myself to a certain kind of tasks only.

But as years passed a strong history of this dreaded disease cancer started taking roots in our family. First my maternal aunt, then one of my cousins followed by my mother... All had to undergo the pains of Breast Cancer. My Father also suffered from Prostate Cancer. At the back of my mind, I started having this strong belief that one day I would also have to face this demon. Considering this notion my loving husband, Dinesh

Dhawan decided getting my Mammography done once a year as soon as I touched 40 years of age. But however careful you are, sometimes fate plays its role more strongly... At the age of 42, I got my Mammography done and the results were normal. Then after some months I started feeling a lump in my right breast. Due to some unavoidable circumstances in my family and job (Teacher at DPS) commitments I kept postponing my check-up.

In October 2010, I got an off from my job on a working day and I decided to visit my CGHS dispensary. The Lady Doctor touched the area of breast from outside and seemed worried. She asked to get the FNAC done immediately.

I went straight away to the National Institute of Cancer Prevention and Research, Noida and got my sampling done. The result was to be given after two days. After two days, on Karvachauth, I went to the centre alone to collect my report, after my school got over. As I reached there and asked for my report, the person made me sit and handed me the report. The result of FNAC suggested an infiltrating duct carcinoma meaning cancer. We approached Dharamshila Hospital for the treatment. Whole body PET CT (28/10/2010) suggested Cancer Stage IV in Right Breast, axillary lymph nodes, skeletal lesions.

I don't know how, I was very composed when the report was handed to me and I enquired from the person who handed me the reports about the good hospitals that I should approach. He gave me a few names and I left the place.

After coming out of the National Institute of Cancer Prevention and Research, Noida I called up my husband and then I lost all my control and burst into tears. He consoled me and asked me to reach home and joined me soon. We felt devastated for a few hours. Finally, my husband composed himself and made me feel very comfortable.

The treatment that began in 2010, was of chemotherapy for 9 cycles and lasted for about one and a half years. Then oral medication followed with PET-CT every six months to monitor the disease.

Again, fate played its role and in April 2014 the disease recurred. This time we came to Max Hospital, Patparganj as Dr. Meenu Walia had joined Max Hospital. As advised by her I again went through 6 cycles of chemotherapy. Dr. Meenu Walia further advised Oral medicines and PET-CT every 6 months for regular monitoring.

Everything went smoothly for 5 years. In August 2019 the disease cropped up again. Dr. Meenu Walia keeping herself updated with new developments in the treatment started my treatment with targeted therapy, which is going on till date.

The most difficult part initially was to disclose the news to my sons. My dear husband was the only one who was with me for all my support. He stood by me religiously in every way ... never expressing his issues vocally!

Gradually weakness and fatigue began physically. Still I continued with my job. My husband's continuous moral and physical support kept me going.

After the disease developed the second time, it was becoming difficult to continue with my job. Still I kept going for a while because it kept me busy mentally also and so I didn't have the time to think about my problem. After a year in 2015 I told my husband casually that I wanted to leave my job and as always he understood my situation and helped me in taking this decision.

The key to my motivation and determination is my husband. Nobody in the house discussed cancer in front of me. He never let me feel that I had any problem and the atmosphere in the house was normal. He knew very well that to keep me motivated, my mind needed to remain occupied. He got printouts of stories where people have gone to their job after their chemo sessions. This helped me a lot and I even continued with my job in a normal way, except for the days when I had to go for chemo.

In my school I told my colleagues in my department about it and requested them not to spread the news. I wanted to work normally and did not want the children I was teaching to have any different feelings for me. My colleagues supported me, and I tried to accomplish all the tasks the same way as I did earlier.

After my chemo sessions got over my husband planned a trip to Himachal. His determination that I could travel, and I am absolutely normal kept me motivated. Then after a year we went to Kashmir and Leh in the chilling winter of December-January. All these trips kept infusing a strong belief that "Life is beautiful if you live it beautifully." On our 25th Marriage Anniversary in 2016, after my first reoccurrence of the disease, my husband took me to North East India to spend memorable holidays!!! We also went to Khajuraho and Orcha the same year.

My sons Aakarsh and Utkarsh have constantly been with me physically and emotionally. Whenever required they accompany me for my hospital visits. As I am fond of movies, they keep planning and book tickets for movies very often. Aakarsh orders books for reading showing that he is interested in reading them. But I know he is doing this for me. I am blessed to have such a beautiful family!!!

My husband made this horrible disease bearable. He made it almost impossible to be sad. He keeps me so positive and keeps my mind completely off it. When I get sad, he is so unbelievably comforting. He almost took my sickness away by doing everything he could to take away the pain. He lets me rest, take care of the children, cooks food, even when he has to go to work.

He took off work all the time to care for me. He took me to my appointments, which are sometimes every day, all day. He has stayed with me throughout every hospital stay. He researched my medications, he researched all he could to help me beat this. He convinced me every time on how beautiful I am without my hair. When my disease reoccurred in 2014, he decided to go for a Photo Session, before I lose my hair again...

The second most important person in my Journey of this Special Time is Dr. Meenu Walia. Her patience to listen to your problems and ever smiling face is very assuring. As soon as I step into her room and sit with her, I start feeling comfortable and have very strong feeling that I am in Safe Hands. She is a brilliant researcher, empathetic, humane and her calm and poised nature works as a soothing ointment for ailing minds. She discusses the various options of treatment at any stage whenever required and guides for the proper treatment.

The staff associated with Dr. Meenu Walia is super supportive. Be it Mr. Azad, Sister Kavita, Sister Jessy and many others, who always greet you with a smile. They are just a phone call away and help to guide for various tasks like appointment, tests, etc.

Max Healthcare is the axis around which my life is moving smoothly medically. It has been very satisfying from the very first day I stepped in. The distribution of various jobs among staff members has been very helpful and approachable. In the course of the Oncology treatment, I also came up with the issue of hernia. I am really very thankful to Dr. Bachan Singh Barthwal for my successful surgery. He was very gentle and made me very comfortable to discuss my problems. He had consultation with Dr. Meenu Walia as well about my problem to decide for the course of treatment. It is the excellent teamwork of various departments in a good hospital like Max Healthcare that is very helpful for a patient's treatment.

Attitude towards life has changed a lot. Before, life was very busy juggling between the household and job responsibilities. Never thought of giving time to self or enjoy the company of husband and children. After, I realized the importance of each moment of life. Try my best to have a good time with my close ones, cherishing every sweet moment and unbound joy. To keep myself engaged my husband again came to my rescue. He motivated me to create YouTube Channel and Create and Upload videos. So, now I have Channels of Classical Music in which my husband gives his music contribution and a Cookery Channel. This keeps me so busy that the thought of my problem rarely comes to my mind.

The first and foremost thought that I want to share with everyone is, never neglect your medical problems. Give it your first priority to get the check-ups done if feeling any problem. Secondly, if diagnosed with a dreadful disease, try to stay stable mentally. This helps in your treatment and recovery and also gives a positive energy to your caretaker. To stay strong mentally, you can get strength from believing in God and reading scriptures. Reading stories of various cancer survivors who are leading an almost normal life can also give you mental strength.

Change your priorities in life. Appreciate life more. Help other people in any way that you can. Reorganize your life and set new goals. Don't blame God, "Why me?" There must have been many happy moments in your life... Did you ask at that time "Why me?"

Last but not the least, don't expect much from your extended family. They have their own life, and your problem is going to take time to leave, and so it is not justified to expect them to come to your rescue. There will be plenty of advice pouring in from friends, relatives and whatsapp messages. Don't follow them blindly. Discuss with your doctor and then take a decision.

❑

Stella Singh

| 54/F | Endometrial Stromal Sarcoma | 2015

I, Stella Singh hailing from Lucknow. I would like to share my experience with you. I have been facing this disease (cancer) for the past one year. Initially I did not have any pain when I consulted a doctor though I had abdominal discomfort persistently. The doctor asked me to get a USG done. After seeing the report, the doctor told me that I had cancer. I cannot explain in words what I was going through emotionally. After that I got a CT scan done and all the tests were indicative of cancer. My whole family was tense.

We spent 15 days at Tata Memorial Hospital, Mumbai and came back disappointed. We took multiple opinions in Lucknow but all of them told us that surgery is very risky, and anything can happen. Then Dr. Chandrawati operated me, but the problem persisted despite surgery. Ultrasound showed relapse of the tumour and again the series of opinions started.

Finally, in December we reached Max Hospital PPG. I underwent surgery in January. I was told to undergo chemotherapy. For which I met Dr. Meenu Walia. After profiling I was initiated on Oral tablets.

My entire family was very supportive throughout this time. My family took care of me and the faith and belief in God kept me going. Because whenever I was tense and depressed, I used to read the Bible and pray to almighty. I am very satisfied and happy with the support I get from my family.

❑

Usha Rani

| 53/F | CA Ovary | 2015

Every person goes through many highs and lows in life. One must learn to embrace these moments and make the best out of them. I learnt the same when I was diagnosed with cancer in January 2015.

Initially, I had urine infection. I got myself tested at Max Hospital and then I came to know that I was suffering from Ovary and Uterus Cancer, Stage Ill.

Like any other person, I too was shocked end depressed. It felt like someone snatched the ground beneath me and I thought this was the end of my life. But when you have a loving family to support you, you know that only good things will happen to you. They told me not to worry as treatments are available and I would be fine soon.

So, I filled my mind with positivity and automatically all the positive people started surrounding and motivating me. I started my treatment at Max Hospital where Dr. Harit, Dr. Meenu and Dr. Arora along with the nurses provided me with the best treatment during my journey of 6 months. In fact, the care and support provided to me by the staff helped me recover faster.

My daughter and son-in-law helped me a lot during this journey. After the treatment I love my life more than ever and wish to live longer. And today, I'm back to living my life to the fullest, leaving all my problems behind. I have emerged as a stronger, happier, more cheerful woman. Cancer taught me to challenge the challenges life throws at you...

❑

SECTION - III

Veteran Champions Stories

Anju Jain

| 60/F | CA Pancreas | 2019

Life was a roller coaster journey for this Economics professor. Mother of three grown up children and wife of a successful and devoted doctor, she hardly had time to look back.

2018 came as a turning point in her life. She had been feeling uneasy since August and was having problems with digestion. Initially thought to be food poisoning, it turned out to be something else. An ultrasound and other tests in the month of November said that all was not well. Reports revealed cancer head of pancreas.

It came as a big shock for the family as it was least expected. The disease was diagnosed at Metro Hospital, Noida, but as treatment required specialization, some hospitals were shortlisted.

Max Patparganj was the nearest good hospital. Through reference Dr. P. K. Mishra was consulted for surgery. Surgery was conducted on December 12, 2018 but the tumour could not be removed. On advice of Dr. Mishra, Dr. Meenu Walia was consulted and thus began the treatment under her. Getting an efficient doctor is very important in this disease and it is where God helped us.

2019 was really bad as there were long hospitalizations in ICU and HDU. Many times, there were breaks in chemo treatment. Cycles of folforinox were planned for her. Overall, it was a difficult year. She was put on oral medicine. As some traces were found in the liver a new treatment plan was devised for her.

There was some relief in 2020. Now her treatment continues at Max Vaishali Day Care. Dr. Walia and her team have been extremely considerate and affectionate. She personally monitors all her patients and has groomed her team very well. I wish to express my gratitude to her and each member of her team.

As a caregiver, I would like to draw attention towards the following points:

- Early detection is important. Listen to your body.
- For onco problem, it is pertinent to shortlist a hospital where treatment can be continued for long.
- Family members need a total change in outlook as it is almost like a battle against might.
- Go for a good doctor through reference.
- It is very painful for the patient, so family members please be tolerant.
- Positivity and spirituality proved to be time tested my friends.
- Mrs. Ila Bhushan (Sister of Mrs. Anju Jain)

❑

Ashok Kumar Jain

| 63/M | NHL | 2007

I was diagnosed with NHL Lymphoma in November 2007. I came across the situation when, my barber during massage informed me that there was a certain lump on my neck. I never got to notice it because it was painless. Further, to get the medical consultation for the same, I visited an ENT specialist near my hometown. He advised me some medication to subside that node but a few months later it was again there in the same condition and that time he advised me to consult an oncologist.

After discussing my situation with some of the known ones, I got to know about Dr. Meenu Walia. I immediately took made an appointment and got some tests done as advised by her. After analysing the reports, she confirmed cancer of Non-Hodgkin's Lymphoma. After knowing the diagnosis, I went into shock. I was simply not ready to accept my reports therefore, I shared my reports with another lab and from there also I got back with the same results. Having gained my trust in Dr. Meenu Walia, I went back to her where she handled my stressed state very well and guided me to go through a proper treatment.

Her motivation worked wonders for me, and I got the strength to fight with my disease. The treatment was 8 long cycles of chemotherapy which left me drained with side-effects. In the beginning, my TLC was falling, due to which my body temperature rose, and I suffered infection and loose motions. But later I adjusted with chemotherapy and completed my cycles successfully. The efficient team of my doctors supported me thoroughly during chemotherapy and they provided me aids to handle side-effects and enabled me to tolerate chemos.

Most importantly, during my crucial time my wife stood firmly by my side and helped me sail through the battle of cancer. Since, my children were abroad that time, so she was the sole family figure who acted as my backbone and took care of me day and night. Moreover, my office colleagues and friends also kept me motivated and happy during my tough times. I consider this as my sheer luck to have got treated by highly qualified and professional team of doctors of Max Hospital and other support staff who provided me homely care in my hard times.

Now, I am retired from my bank job and leading a peaceful life by associating myself with social activities of helping the needy and poor people.

❑

Damodar Prasad

| 72/M | CA Sigmoid Colon | 2014

It all started when I noticed blood coming with the stool. I consulted my CGHS doctor about this and he told me that it could be piles. He advised me to go to a hospital and find out its reason. I went to GTB and there I found that it was colon cancer. I got myself tested and admitted in GTB, but I was a beneficiary of CGHS, so I shifted to Max Hospital. My surgery was done on May 26, 2014. After that I came to the Oncology Department under Dr. Meenu Walia and carried on with chemotherapy.

When I came to know that I am affected by cancer the first thought was that I would not live anymore. I will die. I was upset about the test results. When meeting Dr. Meenu Walia my eyes were filled with tears. I was very sad knowing that it is cancer, and it is impossible for my survival. But Dr. Walia explained to me that nothing will happen "Baba" and you will be all right.

Under her treatment I became well. I cannot forget her as she gave me a new life. It will be now 7 years since I was operated for surgery and after that underwent 6 cycles of chemotherapy. Now, I come for follow up.

Dr Meenu Walia and her team treated me very well and saved my life. I think whatever I am it is only for their grace.

The doctors and their staff are like God or divinity for me. I thank them profusely. My family members specially my wife also helped me tremendously in the hard times.

Now that I am a cancer survivor, I feel that one should be firm to fight any difficulty and any disease happily. The disease will be ended. The power will automatically come out to fight the disease.

My life really changed from an ailing person to a healthy person. Previously I was a cancer patient and now I think that I am healthy after the excellent treatment given by my doctor.

❑

G. C. Saxena

| 60/M | AML | 2010

I am G. C. Saxena from New Delhi. My health started deteriorating from September 2010 and my body used to feel low and down all through the day. I consulted few doctors regarding the same, but there was no considerable improvement in my state. Due to the continuous decline, I was admitted to Tirath Ram Hospital on November 6, 2010 where I went through a pathology test. After examining the blood report, the doctor suggested I should consult an Oncologist. My family doctor recommended Dr. Meenu Walia. Before meeting her, I was totally unaware about my disease, but I had a clue that something serious was going on with me.

I met Dr. Meenu Walia without any delay, and she advised me to get admitted for a few tests. Later, I was diagnosed with

AML (Blood cancer). I was shocked with the name cancer and started thinking what had happened to me. My family members were also so tense and worried with the reports but later Dr. Meenu Walia briefed us about AML and supported me with her guidance. She motivated me that this disease is curable if I complete my treatment and even discussed some Do's and Don'ts about this disease which helped me get cured faster. She advised chemotherapy as a treatment, which we started without any delay.

During my chemo, my family especially my son, sailed me throughout this battle. He always stood by my side and kept me boosted with his support and positive attitude. I used to pray to God for my recovery. I usually spent my time reading books during the chemo sessions.

After a few cycles of chemo, I found myself recovering, my strength and my will power started to grow again. I became more positive and always followed the guidance of Dr. Walia. I was very conscious about my diet.

I thank Dr. Meenu Walia, who added a few more moments to my life, I am also thankful to all her team members who helped me in fighting cancer. I will never forget the services of Max Hospital and their way of treating patients with cancer.

I am a survivor now and regularly following up with my doctor. I have also resumed my daily activities with a healthy lifestyle.

❑

Indira Mathur

| 64/F | CA Breast | 2007

In the year 2007, I felt a lump formation in my right breast. I told my husband about it and decided to contact a doctor immediately. My cousin is a cardiologist and we talked to him on the phone and took an appointment with him. He checked me and advised me to go for mammography. Till then we were not aware of this test at all. We went to a testing lab in Patel Nagar. They did the mammography and then talked to Dr. Mathur. He, thereafter, advised us to go to a cancer hospital.

We opted for Dharamshila Hospital. We went there and were directed to Dr. Niranjan Naik. Dr. Naik saw me and did a FNAC test. He advised us to go for surgery. We immediately agreed. This he planned for the next day only. He asked us, if needed could he remove the breast? We agreed and the operation was performed the next day. We were then directed to Dr. Meenu Walia, who was our Medical Oncologist. She advised us to go for chemotherapy. The sessions were to be done at an interval of 21 days each. This time was very critical.

I am a very optimistic person and had the confidence that everything would be fine. My family also supported me immensely. This process was long, lasting for 8-9 months. This was testing time, but I have great faith in God.

Praying every day also gave me strength to withstand this ordeal. I would get a feeling that everything would be all right. I would get well. I have to look after my two daughters. God is kind and will ensure that I will be fine after these chemotherapies. Self-confidence, faith in my destiny and confidence in God gave me immense strength to withstand this process.

Today it is over 14 years and I feel fine. Dr. Meenu Walia also supported me and took good medical care during this period. God willing everything is satisfactory today.

❑

Kamaljeet Kaur

| 61/F | CA Breast | 2003

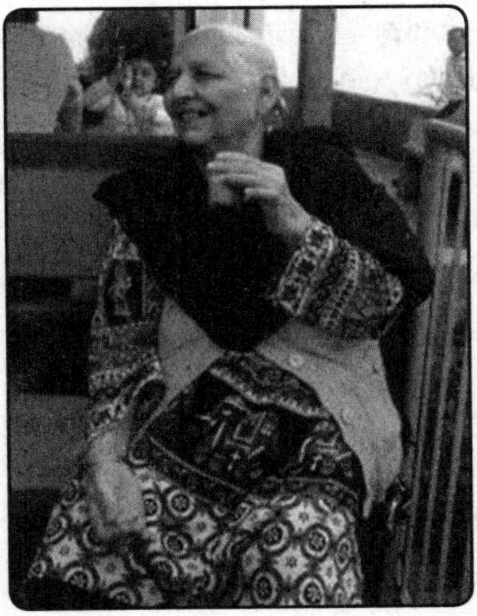

My first experience with breast cancer was in 2003. I noticed some itching in my underarm and ignored for a year. I wasn't very concerned. I discussed it with my sister. She advised me and my children to consult a doctor.

Without delay, I consulted my family doctor and he referred me to consult an oncologist. Despite maintaining sound health throughout my life, for years, I felt that a cancer diagnosis was coming my way.

I came to know about cancer after my surgery in 2004. I came to know about the disease when my breast has been removed. I was diagnosed with stage 3 breast cancer. That time I was very upset and shocked and broken to pieces. I was overwhelmed and scared about my family and children's future. But later, I was counselled that the disease is curable if treatment is taken properly. After that, I got new energy to fight with cancer.

After the consultation with Dr. Meenu Walia my treatment plan was set up for 6 cycles of chemotherapy followed by radiation therapy. It was a tough time for us, as my husband was also patient of hypertension, undergoing treatment and my children were studying that time, we had gone through a financial crisis. But still my treatment was first priority for my family.

The hardest part of going through cancer treatment was actually the fear. I knew that I had to combat the fear in order to get through treatment—that resisting the fear was somehow part of the treatment. That was the mental battle, and for me it was harder than the physical battle. I had to rely completely on my religious faith in order to have the strength to fight the battle of my life.

I was bed-ridden for 2 years during my treatment; my whole family was affected mentally and financially. But my strong belief in God gifted me another healthy life. My husband and children supported me and motivated me to achieve new life. I was in the right hands of Dr. Meenu Walia, who supported me through the treatment.

In all, my experience of interacting with medical staff and others that I have met had been a positive one. I hope I have a number of years before me which, in part, is so far due to the encouragement I experience from my family. With a strong belief in God and doctor you can always win in fighting with cancer because I heard somewhere on the earth, doctors are also born to give new life.

I want to tell everyone to have positivity and faith in God so that you beat a disease like cancer. Today, I am on follow up since 2006 and leading a healthy life. I live happily with my family.

❑

K.P.K. Nambissan

| 62/M | Metastatic Melanoma | 2015

I am a retired deputy secretary from the Dept. of Personnel and Training Government of India. After a successful career of 37 years, I settled in Mayur Vihar, Phase 1 with my wife. She was also working as section officer in Doordarshan. I was waiting for her retirement in 2016 for getting settled in our hometown in Kerala. At the time of retirement in March 2013 I was comfortable, and my two male children were in comfortable positions. The elder one is an IT engineer and settled in USA with his family and younger one is an MBA from IIT Ahmedabad working as a consultant in a company. During the year 2015, our new home was being constructed in my hometown in Calicut with the hope that we would settle there in 2017. In the year 2014, while taking a bath, I noticed a black mole of 1 cm in diameter on my right heel. It continued to remain there for about nine months without giving any trouble.

With the passage of time, it grew in size about 2cm in diameter. This was followed by roughening of the skin surface with 2, 3 holes. A few drops of blood used to come in the morning while walking and mild pain was there. I consulted my family doctor who diagnosed it as a cone and advised for minor surgery. In the meanwhile, I also consulted homeopathy doctor in Kerala, he advised me for medicine treatment about 3 months by which I got minor relief.

But later again I found blood from the mole and consulted a surgeon in Max Noida for surgery. Here it was diagnosed as an infected wart and underwent excision conservation of the lesion in September 2015. Later I noticed swelling in the right groin and my surgeon advised me for FNAC which was done in October 2015. Test result was suggestion of metastatic tumour with possibility of metastatic melanoma. I was referred to Oncologist Dr. Meenu Walia, who advised me for PET CT scan and biopsy through which it was confirmed to Metastatic melanoma and PET scan showed inguinal lymph node.

Later I was advised for surgery after chemotherapy. During chemotherapy, I felt challenges related to side effects of the treatment such as loss of appetite, vomiting, hair loss and low immunity. I was totally cut off from family and friends' circles. My faith in God helped me to overcome the challenges. I used to console myself by reading spiritual texts of great masters and chanting the names of God innumerable times with the hope that God would show me a way out of the predicament.

My wife and children were ready to make any sacrifice for my survival. They always gave me courage and coordinated well and successfully in the treatment with doctors.

❑

Mohinder Duggal

| 83/F | Uterine and Breast Cancer | 2018

In 2018, my mother was diagnosed with Stage 1 Cancer of the Uterus and Stage 2 Breast Cancer (Dual Primary Cancers).

The very first symptom was vaginal bleeding. The point of worry was that my mother is 84 years old (83 at that time) and vaginal bleeding was unusual. This, however, wasn't the first instance. When it had happened three months back (in August 2018) none of the tests revealed anything but muscle atrophy. This time however, we went and sought the advice of a gynaecologist at B.L. Kapoor Hospital, but they also did not provide a definite diagnosis but hinted at cancer. We went to other doctors and got ultrasounds done. A definite diagnosis was given at Max Hospital, Vaishali where ultimately her treatment including surgery was conducted.

More shocking was the fact that all this while we thought the problem was in the uterus, but she also had malignant nodes in one of the breasts. This was revealed in the PET Scan. There were no symptoms of the breast cancer and hence it never came to our attention or to the attention of previous doctors. Dr. Meenu Walia supervised our case at Max Hospital.

My mother and the entire family were nervous as one would naturally expect. This meant many sleepless nights and ambiguity over the success of the treatment. This is not to exaggerate but we truly believe that we wouldn't have been hopeful, nor would have been my mother if it wasn't for the encouragement and hope given to us by Dr. Walia and her entire medical and surgical team. When the diagnosis was made it was during the wedding of her grandson. However, she attended all the functions and without any discomfort only because of the care, medicines and encouragement given by each and every member of the team.

Surgery and the subsequent radiation and targeted therapy took one year. It specifically took more time because her doses were diluted and given once every week due to my mother's age.

The slight pain and bleeding in between medicines was a discomfort for my mother as she is an arthritis patient and could not move around much. The fear was crippling besides everything and that was the biggest hardship. Another worrisome issue was that she had to go through two major surgeries on the same day and at the same time and there was uncertainty regarding the effect of the anaesthetic medicine due to her age and that she is a diabetic patient.

We would always tell her how confident her doctors were regarding her treatment. Another source of motivation came from the fact that during every visit of the hospital we would encounter different cancer patients with unusual case histories and all of them would talk at length about their revival journey and how we were in competent hands. That was the biggest factor that kept us afloat when we were drowning in worry.

We convey our heartfelt thanks to Dr. Meenu Walia, Dr. Geeta, Dr. Kanika Gupta, Dr. Sanjeev Arora, Dr. Sandeep

Aggarwal, Dr. Rashi and all the junior doctors and staff members for all their support during this ordeal.

We wandered around with my mother's reports going from one hospital to another or one clinic to another. We don't think that we would have received the level of heathcare (pre-op and post-op) that we did at Max Hospital. We were also getting the treatment through the CGHS Card and we never faced any issue or harassment regarding the card.

She is a diabetic and arthritis patient and for all specific disorders she was suffering from, a different doctor was brought on board, and all of them treated us with respect and care. Every doctor would engage my mother in the treatment plan, and she would actively discuss her previous medical histories. Cancer rather than becoming a taboo which will not be discussed in the household, became the centre of most conversations which my mother would steer making sure all her reports were properly discussed with the doctors and kept properly.

It is very hard to be positive in these trying times, but all we have to do is consciously try to stay positive, be hopeful and optimistic. The more our happy cells are increased, the more we gain strength to get through the struggle and toll our body goes through. In general, also we need to always try to remain positive and be hopeful. If our mind is happy and healthy, our bodies will replicate the same.

Mentally and emotionally, we have become stronger after seeing a first-hand experience. The courage of family and love helped us to go through this and uplift our morale. Health-wise, we have become more aware of my body and taken a healthy lifestyle more seriously. We focus more on things that make us happy and follow a discipline. We are fortunate to be given another chance and should be grateful every day.

❑

Neeta Rani

| 67/F | Multiple Myeloma | 2015

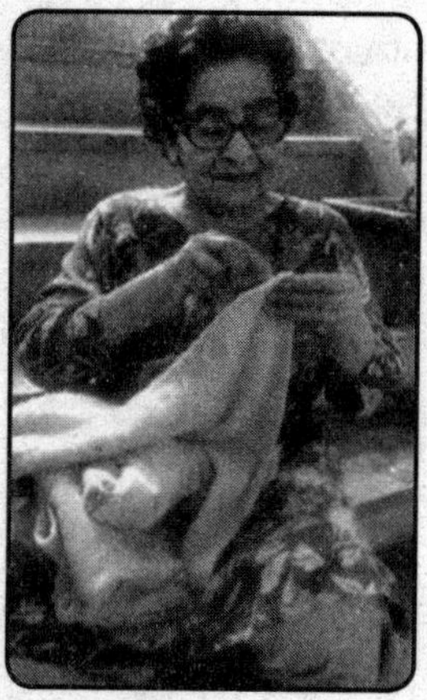

I was diagnosed in May 2015. I presented with complaints of severe backache and inability to walk. I went to a local hospital but did not get any relief. Later I consulted a neurosurgeon and was advised PET CT and I was diagnosed to be suffering from Multiple Myeloma.

That time I was completely shocked by knowing the diagnosis. I had always been a hard worker all my life and suddenly realized that I could not work at all or even stand properly. I had become totally bed-ridden and dependent on my family members even for my basic needs. That time I prayed to god to grant me death. I did not want to spend the rest of my life bedridden as a burden on my family members.

Somebody advised me about Max Hospital and Dr. Meenu Walia for my treatment. When I met Dr. Meenu Walia this is when my life changed. I started with my treatment and kept praying to God either grant me a cure or death. It was my luck that I met Dr. Meenu Walia.

Dr Meenu Walia and her entire team were very supportive. Even my family members supported me a lot; they always stood by my side. I went through chemotherapy and was supported by my doctor and her team.

Now I am glad that I am able to work and be self-dependent again with the treatment under my doctor.

❑

P. K. Chaddha

| 64/F | CA Breast | 2014

The day, I was diagnosed with cancer, my family and I were completely shocked. It shattered my faith and the world came tumbling down in front of me. The very first question came to my mind was "Why Me"? "What have I done?" but ultimately no answer for this. I wept, I cried, I scolded myself but all-in vain.

I had a very healthy and beautiful life. I was working as an officer in the Government of India and just after retirement I got this shock. But there was no option other than to accept it, but with strong will power and a positive attitude, the almighty God, my family and my friends and of course to expert, sincere, affectionate and motivation by Dr. Meenu Walia and Dr. Harit and the whole team of the Cancer Department at Max Hospital Patparganj, I recovered and won over this disease.

God helps those who help themselves and where there is a will there is a way. The doctors, family, friends and support helped me to cross the wild sea. It is very difficult to bear the cuts, scars, change of skin colour on top of that loss of hair, behaviour of the people Oh My God I can't explain...

I just want to give a message to the society, though it is very difficult to cross this, dreadful and drastic phase but it is not impossible to achieve the goal.

Cancer is curable, but we have to identify our all-support systems and stay away from the negative thoughts and people.

Timely diagnosis and under the supervision of experts, doctors and staff, supportive family and faith in yourself and God will help to achieve the target.

I was fortunate enough to have all these and under the expert advice and treatment of Max Hospital, I am out of this danger.

Fight against the cancer with will power and positive attitude. Never give up.

It is your choice to be a victim or survivor.

❑

Padam Paras Sharma

| 73/F | CA Ovary | 2014

My name is Padam Paras Sharma. I have retired from the Ministry of Defense. Currently I am 75 years old. In November 2014 my left leg started to swell and pain. For a few days I tried to ignore it but later I consulted my family doctor who advised me to get the FNAC test, reports of which confirmed cancer. Then I met Dr. Meenu Walia in Dharamshila Hospital. She advised me to get a PET CT scan. With the result of PET CT, I was diagnosed with ovarian cancer with stage 3. My family and I were totally shocked, and I was really depressed. Then Dr. Meenu Walia motivated me to get the treatment started. My children helped me to get stronger and then I decided that I have to beat cancer.

Chemotherapy started and it was very tough for me to tolerate chemotherapy. I got used to face the side-effects. Many times, I was rushed to hospital in emergency and I had to be taken on a stretcher most of the time. After 4 cycles of chemotherapy, Dr. Pankaj and Dr. Alok performed surgery on me which was really very painful. I used to stay in hospital more than at home. My son Ratnesh Sharma sailed me through this battle of cancer as he was with me all the time. My daughter supported us all the way. They both continuously motivated me to get through. Dr. Meenu Walia was the one who treated me on all occasions and got me through every time.

After the surgery, 2 cycles of chemotherapy were given to me, which were very tough. It took one year to get all the treatment done and the last chemo finished in July 2015. I had always set my mind that I have to get well sooner. I kept praying to God for my life and believed that whatever God had destined for us will happen and we have to perform our duties and fight every obstacle.

I am glad that I was again able to stand on my feet and work individually. I especially thank Max Hospital who stood by me and provided great support, care and excellent treatment.

❑

Rajeshwari Tripathi

| 60/F | Adenocarcinoma Lung | 2010

I remember the day when my wife Rajeshwari Tripathi was diagnosed with lung cancer in 2010 when she suffered intense chest pain.

When I look at my wife... Lung Cancer is certainly not something that comes to my mind. But people exactly like her are the new faces of this disease. My wife knew that something was wrong as she felt weak, sick and had pronounced shortness of breath, and a chronic cough. As a non-smoker lung cancer was not the immediate consideration for her doctors.

We directly moved to Dr. Meenu Walia for her treatment. She jotted some notes in her medical profile to check for lung cancer. My wife was losing hope to fight this disease, but Dr. Walia turned out to be the positive and strong turning point in her life.... She said... "Your life is not important to anyone as it is to you... you really have to stand up for yourself".

My wife was willing to go for chemotherapies after Dr. Walia made her understand the treatment process very patiently. She underwent every line of treatment suggested by the doctor. Now she is not just surviving but living a good quality of life.

It was not easy for my wife. She had gone through the bouts of fear, anxiety and disappointment on the way back to her wellness and recovery. She was scared but Dr. Walia was the only inspiration and encouragement for her. She has always supported her and listened to her very patiently whenever she was in pain. She was so happy that Dr. Walia had made her fall into the category of cancer survivor and determined to stay cancer-free.

Finding a good doctor is very important and hard to get, this is exactly I was thinking before meeting Dr. Walia. But she has amazingly supported her and even my family. I am grateful to her for every day she has given to my wife.

Honestly, being a cancer survivor has been both educational and horrific! Still, my wife feels blessed by all the love, support and the quality of medical care that she has received from Dr. Meenu Walia and her team.

❑

Ram Chander

| 70/M | NHL | 2017

During the second week of March 2017, I noticed one gland in my right thigh on the upper side. I went to Dr. Virendra Gupta, MS (Surgery) for treatment. Dr. Gupta advised me to take the FNAC test and the report suspected high-grade Non-Hodgkin's Lymphoma.

My son Sushil suggested that I should contact Dr. Meenu Walia for check-up and further advice. Dr. Meenu Walia after examining me advised for further tests which confirmed the symptoms of NHL and advised for chemotherapy. Before going for chemotherapy, I was briefed about side-effects of chemo. I was told that not all patients have side-effects. I made up my mind, why can't I be a non-side effect patient?

This gave me inner support and I began my complete treatment under Dr. Meenu Walia.

After the 4th cycle I was advised for a PET CT and the report showed favourable treatment response. Treatment continued till the 8th cycle and the PET CT done after it showed pelvic lymph nodes were no longer FDG avid. After the 2nd PET CT scan, I was again assured and told that I need not worry and will be

100% fit after completion of the full treatment which encouraged and reassured me.

Now I am on follow-up treatment and I am progressing well and feeling completely stress-free. I am a cancer survivor.

❑

Sulekh Chand Jain

| 74/M | CA Colon | 2017

I felt a pain in my abdomen and consulted a general physician. He prescribed me some medicines and I kept on taking those, however I continued to feel extremely weak and lethargic. This went on for around 3-4 months. Once I was carrying some household objects when I suddenly fell down all of a sudden. My children were with me and they were shocked. This incident made us think more seriously about my condition.

Finally, after consulting several other doctors and getting multiple tests done, I arrived at Dr. Meenu Walia's OPD in May 2017. She advised further tests and my blood investigations were suggestive of anaemia. My colonoscopy and further scans were also done which reported that I had a tumour in the large intestine. I was diagnosed to have cancer of the intestine, which is also known as colon cancer.

A cancer diagnosis at the age of 74 is something that no one expects. My family was not prepared for this. It came as a big shock for all of us. But, I am a religious man and I am always positive. I knew things would change, for there is no disease that is not curable. I had a firm belief in almighty God and my treating doctors and got ready to start my treatment.

Dr Meenu sympathetically and graciously told not to worry as today the cure for cancer is possible with success. She suggested that I should go for surgery first, so she referred me to a surgeon. My surgery went smoothly and I did not have any complications after it. Later, my chemotherapy started. I was fortunate that I did not have any significant side-effects of chemo as well. I completed my treatment successfully in January 2018 and since then go for regular follow-ups.

But life did not stop for me at cancer diagnosis. I am very thankful to Dr. Meenu Walia and her team for bringing him back to life and normal routine. Being the religious nature, I never went under depression and I diverted myself in religious activities and started studying Jain religion literature. During the day I remained busy studying and writing poetry. In hospital also I composed beautiful poems and one on Dr. Walia's pleasing nature with patients.

I am a civil engineer by profession, now retired. At the age of 74 I changed my mind to learn ancient languages Sanskrit and Prakrit. By God's grace in 2018 I got admission to the LBS Sanskrit Central University Delhi for BA (Sanskrit and Praktri). In 2021 I successfully passed. Today I am 78 and now on the path of completing MA and PhD in Jain Darshan.

Cancer couldn't stop me. I always made myself believe that I don't have cancer. My courage and self-motivation throughout the treatment helped me win this battle. The aim is to remain cheerful under all circumstances for a stress-free enjoyable life.

❑

SECTION - IV

Power Couple Stories

Anushila Bhattacharya

| CA Ovary | 2014

Prabuddha Bhattacharya

| CA Prostate | 2017

Grandma's philosophy of life was to do what seemed like a good idea at the time and do it as hard as possible. It had never let her down and it is still valid today (dadi *ma ki nuskhe*)

The same strategy was adopted by my parents: *Stay low, stay quiet, keep it simple, don't expect too much, and enjoy what you have...*

Both brilliant in academics, my parents Sri Prabuddha Kr. Bhattacharyya and Smt Anushila Bhattacharya, settled in the Steel Township of Durgapur during the formative days of the eminent city and lived up to the Tag line *'there is a little bit of sail in everybody's life'*.

A State Gold medallist, BE/M.Tech. in Operational Research, he contributed tons in various Department in SAIL both India and abroad and became founder of “Panchabati” society, meaning *abode of 5 Banyan trees*, which is an epitome of togetherness still residing in the hearts of the Steel Township.

With Masters in her kitty, she chose the teaching profession and excelled as Mathematics Lecturer with a huge fan following amongst the student population... a rare feat in this discipline.

Having groomed three children to their respective successful lives, they are now faced with the Demon of modern-age pollution and lifestyle— cancer!!

It was summer of 2014, just after *Baisakhi*. Maa came to Delhi from Kolkata and complained about a projected stomach tissue which looked like hernia. We consulted our family doctor who recommended Gastro HOD at Fortis, who in turn advised CT Scan. The results were horrifying. We were shocked and numbed beyond words. It was our first encounter with cancer and did not know what to do, where to go...the world around us, just stopped spinning! Maa was diagnosed with Ovarian cancer, stage 4.

Baba’s case was highlighted during routine check-up by our family doctor when PSA results were marginally high and consistent for quite long. The first biopsy from the local clinic was null but PSA results continued to be the same. So, we did the second biopsy from Max Patparganj and Prostrate Cancer, stage 2 was detected.

First thought was, O God! Why me?

Both, Baba Maa faced this deadly disease bravely. Initially, after receiving the cancer diagnosis, they were at a loss. The thought of living with cancer and the painful treatment process was extremely overwhelming. We started contacting our relatives, friends, so that they could help with pointers.

Once the hospital and doctors were selected, the next course of action began and became fast paced. Hours turned into days and poured past night; days turned to weeks and so on .... We lost track of time; everything was controlled invisibly; we felt as puppets in the hands of fate. At some point during the treatment Maa felt like giving up hope, but we hung on.

On the onset, one of the reputed hospitals goofed up her case and she went into coma and ventilator support for straight 16 days ... almost lost her! We contacted 5 reputed hospitals in NCR and out-state; except Max Hospital, all other experts gave 4 months' time frame longevity (that was 7 years back).

Both are struggling with the venom for 5.5 years now, but they keep inspiring everyone around them with their energy, vitality and liveliness. There is a 'CAN' in the word 'CANCER' and they are determined to beat it... emphasizing the statement that broken crayons still colour, beautifully.

My mother had to be hospitalized 27 times (chemotherapy mainly). There were moments of desperation; fear of losing her loomed around in the dark corners of our mind. At one night in ICU, I remember standing hopeless...praying to God... Baba had m-o-n-t-h-s of hospitalization due to radiation therapy and he bore all the sessions, sportingly.

The doctors (**Dr. Meenu Walia and team**) stood by us like a rock and *held our hand* steadily guiding us with innovative treatment interventions, detailed planning, and attending to all emergencies with an assuring surety.

The day when Maa got admitted, she was in great pain and discomfort. She had a minor accident that morning when she slipped in the bathroom. We admitted her to one hospital, only to transfer her to Max Patparganj when the situation worsened. By late night she was admitted to ICU and her condition kept going downhill from there. *Both kidney failure, fluid accumulation in both lungs, cardiac dysfunction, comatose...it was such a hopeless, dark situation.* I glued myself to the first floor ICU lounge area for 5 straight days. On 19th April night 2 am, I got a call from the ward boy and rushed inside ICU to find Maa's life signs slipping away!!!!! The doctor on duty (**Dr Shonali**) tried very hard and said to me: *"Dawa nahi Dua ki jaroorat hai"*. I stood numbed and kept looking at the monitor blipping through the life support signs.

After 2 hours the condition was still the same. That early morning Dr. **Sanjeev Arora** jumped into action. The whole day he stayed with my mother, ignoring the fact that it was a Sunday, his day-off, and sacrificing attending his own sister's engagement. His priority was saving my mother's life, in the true sense of the word! Late afternoon the vital stats came under control- it was a triumphant moment for everyone! Such is the dedication of the Onco team!

With Baba we had seen the utmost care Dr. **Arun Verma** took in the Radiation Department. Initially there was a confusion with the reports whereby it was concluded that the cancer has spread to the nodes. The course of action was chalked out in a specific manner. But later on, one of the radiologists countered the prognosis and Dr. **Anand** was called in for review. After MRI and other tests, it came out to be TB. The cancer was localized to the organ and had not spread. This was comforting and the actual treatment began. The whole course went quite smoothly and hassle free. Post treatment results were extremely good, and Baba is happy!

As Children, we cannot speak for Baba-Maa's emotions during the whole journey till remission, but we have seen the pain/ fear/ anticipation/ depression etched on their faces... never expressing vocally but enduring silently!

It is one point in life when you feel the body weight in the literal sense. The bones and muscles are no longer supporting you ; the eyes are failing which calls for cataract operation ; the chemo and radiation is causing havoc to your digestive and excretory systems ; you feel nauseous and dizzy all the time ; the immune system is compromised, so you are packed inside a sterile room like new-born babies (*sans the joy*); you are dependent on maids/nurses/home care folks who are clocking 24/7; so-called relatives and friends circle are flooding you with phone calls but very little actual help!; money is flowing down the drain, burning holes in your pocket; every time you go for a clinical test, your heart beat accelerates and you keep praying to God (*to have a good report*); any small parameter variance buzzes as an alarm (maybe false) - whether the cancer is back or not!

Is this really living? A million-dollar question indeed!

Not to mention the impact on the surrounding family members who have to deal with the daily nitty gritty yet continue the everyday chores of family/school/office/household activities.

But we believed focus and determination is the key. None of us could bring ourselves to the fact that *Death is knocking at the door*. We told ourselves that this is another medical issue which can be resolved by the best hands in Max Hospital team and network. We focused on the tiniest of details and started taking small steps towards recovery.

Nobody in the house, ever discussed cancer in front of Baba-Maa. The discussions were regular ones ... just like any other normal household. We made them feel that it is all right, you will get through, don't worry'. We discussed movies and favourite serials; books, magazines and favourite authors; about our daily life stories at office, school and home. They played cards, celebrated birthdays and festivities with us, guided their grandchildren with maths and physics (they loved to solve challenge problems always); and when they felt better accompanied us to tours and travels to the mountains and green valleys.

Although at the back of the minds the *'dementor'* was lurking but we kept our windows (sic mind) shut.

Throughout the turbulent sail our constant pole star was Dr. **Meenu Walia** and her Onco team. Every time we plagued her with our problems, she listened patiently and assured us with her innovative treatment plans and an ever-smiling face. Words have great power, and her advice gave us immense strength to navigate through the dark alleys and finally pull out of it like a miracle. Her treatment procedure is excellent with minimal side effects and pain. She is a brilliant researcher, an extremely considerate kind doctor, always helping and her calm composure is a soothing balm to the ailing mind. Words fall short to describe her *humane* angle. She guides us through different steps in the cancer treatment and provides effective referral to other specialists in Max Hospital for all other ailments which are quite helpful for managing holistic health. (such as: Cardio/ Pulmonology/ Urology/ Radiation-Therapy/ Neurology/ Orthopedics)

We are wholeheartedly indebted to **Dr. Harit Chaturvedi** too. He was our saviour and gladiator who fought so well through the complex surgery. His expert hands eliminated all the marks and roots from within and mother healed beautifully thereafter. A true cancer specialist in Onco Surgery and Best in Delhi/NCR. Timely referral by him to Dr. Meenu Walia for Chemo at the onset and subsequently when CA 125 dropped from 4795 (April 2014) to 15 (September 2016). Dr. Meenu Walia referred the case back to Dr. Harit Chaturvedi for surgery who executed promptly without any loss of time and in excellent manner. Hats off to his team!

We remember staring at the 9 jars (containing different body organs removed) which was wheeled on a table from the OT, after 6.5 hours of surgery. The incision mark went all the way down from chest to lower abdomen, like a post-mortem subject (*only in this case she is our mother and very much alive*). A horrifying sight but much needed. Post care was tough but mother did well and started shining like new within 2.5 months!

In a similar manner, Dr. Meenu Walia, timely referred Baba's case for Radiation therapy which helped to tackle the disease. We are sincerely grateful to Dr. Arun Verma for taking personal care during treatment period and at OPD too.

We opted for Home Care services from Max and had a favourable experience. They are professionals and took good care of patient.

The last few years have been a game changer for me too. Spending multiple years of time in the world of Terminal Disease Wards, I have felt the meaning of life in a very different way. It cannot be explained, but experienced, only. So, no sermons here. We believe that there are only two days in the year that nothing can be done. One is called yesterday and the other is called tomorrow, so today is the right day to love, believe, do and mostly live. In everyone's life ...before the best friends, spouse and everyone else in between, the first and arguably most important relationship is that with your parents. As kids we are trying to keep that up!

Life has transitioned multi-folds before and after cancer...

Earlier, Baba remained busy with his engineering job, and after retirement he had taken up the role of HOD for the regional engineering college. Mother engaged herself with her mathematics teaching job and tutored many students after retirement. She also ran the huge household extremely efficiently.

Now, they spend 100 percent of their time in each other's company relishing each and every droplet of life, cherishes every sweet moment and unbound joy. They are celebrating their 50th Golden Anniversary together this year and we are all ecstatic with the happiness and flow of love that we experience each day in their company.

A few words from Baba and Maa: To overcome this disease which is so expensive we pray to God that even our deadliest enemies (even if they exist) should not suffer from cancer. You have faced many challenges in life, and I have seen you fight and come out on top. This cancer is no different. You are a fighter and I know you will come out on top as always.

Just to quote Robert Frost, "Stopping by Woods on a Snowy Evening"

"The woods are lovely, dark and deep,

But I have promises to keep,

And miles to go before I sleep,

And miles to go before I sleep."

❑

Ravinder Kaur

| CA Breast | 2013

Dr Jasbir Singh

| CA Urinary Bladder | 2018

It was the end of October 2013 when I noticed a dimple on my right breast. I wanted to avoid letting anyone in my family know about it since my daughter was to get married within a month. However there seemed no other way out. Acute fear gripped me, and all thoughts were in denial mode. Being a very positive person, I could only pray to God to save me from this deadly life-threatening disease.

Life seemed to have come to a stand-still when I had to go for innumerable and painful tests to be done in order to actually become sure of the underlying problems. Consultations with doctors at Pushpanjali Crosslay (now Max Vaishali) and Max Healthcare

Patparganj became a regular feature. As a family we were all shattered not knowing what fate had in store for us. Ultimately the truth was out that I have to go under the knife and face all the consequences. The whole house was topsy-turvy with tears flowing down from everybody's eyes. This diagnosis of cancer brought an emotional turmoil for me and my family. This was the time that I realized that I have to face it bravely and stand tall to overcome it. It was unbearable to see my family in tears for my sake.

Finally, we went to meet Dr. Harit Chaturvedi at Max Saket. No words can be enough to explain the bonding that I share with Dr. Harit. I know him personally since our childhood days at Lucknow. He and my younger brother were school mates. All this was a blessing in disguise.

The positivity and the divine aura of his personality put me at great ease mentally. He explained everything and mentioned that he wanted me to be admitted the very next day. Accordingly, as per his advice we went to meet Dr. Sanjeev Arora at Max PPG. Next day Dr. Harit initiated the surgery since he was to proceed on leave for a fortnight and did not wish to delay it. I got my doubts cleared that before my daughter's wedding I wanted my crowning glory (my hair) intact. He apprised me that my first Chemo would be done before the wedding, but my hair would fall after the second Chemo. Everything went off as planned. The good thing was that my Lymph Nodes were not affected. After the surgery I had to undergo 6 cycles of Chemotherapy under the care of Dr. Randeep Singh. It has been 7 long years that I am fine and still continuing my check-ups with Dr. Harit / Dr. Geeta.

But life is full of struggles and has its own ups and down…

We had plans to go to the US to meet our daughter in September

2018. It is rightly said “Man proposes God disposes”. After all the trauma of my ailment, life gave us another jolt when my husband noticed red colour / blood in his urine. This was just a week before we were scheduled to leave for the US.

We consulted our family doctor and he suggested that we should go for an Ultrasound. On further investigation we had another shock staring at us. Again, Dr. Harit advised us to consult Dr. Puneet Ahluwalia.

The second chapter of hospital visits cropped up. My husband had a tumour in his Urinary Bladder and further investigations were diagnosed with “High Grade Transitional Cell Carcinoma with Lamina Propia Invasion”. All our plans for the US visit were left in the dark.

TURBT was performed on September 6, 2018 at Max PPG followed by six (6) weekly doses of BCG induction between November 6, 2018 to December 11, 2018. As a follow up he is still undergoing routine check cystoscopy and BCG induction as suggested by the doctor.

Life is a roller – coaster ride. Both of us are very supportive of each other and very positive too. We have learnt to fight our own battles strongly and have finally emerged as champions.

Our heartfelt gratitude to Dr. Meenu Walia for giving us this platform to put forth our experience as we went through the journey with the support of our family, friends and awesome support system of the eminent doctors of the Oncology Department at Max Hospital.

❑

Shri Krishan

| CA Esophagus, Vocal Cord and Prostate | 2004, 2008, 2018

Sheela Devi

| CA Breast | 2011

I was 58 years old and working at the Ministry of the Finance, Dept. of Expenditure, looking forward to leading my life happily post-retirement. And then suddenly one day I had an encounter with the word that I had never imagined in my life I would get to listen to...cancer.

It was June 2004, when I felt difficulty in swallowing my food. I consulted my doctor at a government hospital followed by a series of investigations. After a treatment of more than a month they passed on the dictum based on an endoscopy that I had the cancer of the esophagus (food pipe).

The world came crashing down for me. I was totally blank about cancer and my mind was occupied with myths of death. I was worried about my family's future. But then I had no other choice than to hold myself up, be strong and strive to survive for the sake of my family.

I underwent immediate surgery in August 2004. The tumour they removed, weighed about 10-11 kgs. I believed now that the surgery is done, I will definitely get cured and live well. I went through chemotherapy after the surgery, successfully completed my treatment and then continued to be on follow-up at Dharamshila Hospital.

Later, I met Dr. Meenu Walia who with her guidance cleared all my doubts about cancer and gifted me a new life. She counselled me very well and assured me that cancer is curable with treatment.

As if one tryst with cancer wasn't enough, 2008 brought another share of the difficulties. This time I had difficulty in speaking and my voice also changed. After examination I was diagnosed with primary stage cancer of the vocal cord. But this time around my reaction was much more confident. I did not fear cancer this time because I was already aware about the chance of recurrence as doctor advised me during surgery. I was self-motivated and again prepared to fight with cancer. As per the planned treatment I went through 35 cycles of Radiation therapy and thereafter again continued with follow-up.

I felt much better after the treatment and later never thought about cancer and kept myself busy throughout the day. Life continued smoothly, but fate had other plans. July 2011, my better half, Sheela, who stood like a rock beside me when I was dealing with this disease was now going on the road of a role-reversal. It was during one of our usual tea-times, when she complained to me of pain in her breast and feeling of a lump. Without wasting a moment, I immediately took her to the hospital and consulted a doctor. They suggested a mammogram and biopsy and the diagnosis was again the devastating word—cancer.

But strangely, my wife reacted much more strongly than me. I remember, I who was always self-motivated during my encounters with cancer, started weeping when my wife was diagnosed. But she remained absolutely calm and asked "What happened? Why are you so worried? Nothing happens! It will be fine". Her composure gave me the strength and we were once again prepared with our swords to fight against this disease.

Her disease was at an advanced stage and she also had to undergo surgery, chemotherapy and radiation. Luckily, only the area around the lump was removed and she did not have to undergo complete breast removal. In 2018, again I was detected with Primary Prostate Cancer but again I got treated and have overcome this problem.

Together we remained strong and never felt that we were ill. We continued taking the treatment under Dr. Meenu Walia and lived life happily. During chemotherapy she explained all the adverse effects of chemo and advised me to be most careful from infection, also discussed the Do's and Don'ts along with diet and prepared us to fight with cancer. She encouraged us to keep ourselves busy and don't think that we are cancer patients. This principal helped us a lot to win. With her good behaviour and attitude half the disease came to an end.

We are also very grateful to our children and family members who always supported us and kept our morale high. I always believed in the importance of physical activity and could never sit idle at home. I started brisk walking and yoga with physical exercise around more than one hour daily and continue doing it till date. While fighting with cancer we learned never take this disease to heart and keep engaged yourself throughout the day. You must go through meditation, yoga or physical exercise which may help in good quality of life and be concerned about your diet.

Today I am 75 and my wife is 73 and we are leading our lives absolutely normally. We have a very positive outlook and believe that "Cancer could never kill us, but we can kill cancer".

❑

SECTION-V

Beyond Borders Stories

Amina Hutak

| 28/F | CA Right Breast | 2018 | Afghanistan

I used to have fever quite frequently, had lost a lot of weight and my skin became dull... I went to the government hospital and there the doctors did some blood tests. After getting the results they said that we need to do a surgery immediately. Unable to think of anything I agreed for the surgery. After the surgery the doctors removed the nodules from my breast and sent them for investigations, but the results were inconclusive. Then I went for a CT scan, there also nothing was clear. Despite consulting several doctors in Afghanistan, none was able to detect what my problem was...but somewhere I knew that "cancer" has entered my life...

I along with my sister then decided to come to India. We searched over internet and came to Max Hospital for an opinion and met Dr. Meenu Walia. I was scared and worried about what would happen next. Before coming to India, I told my family back in Afghanistan to keep my grave ready... what should be done for my funeral... who all to invite... All this because in our country there is no facility to cure cancer and death is all that we had seen.

Dr Meenu Walia started my treatment and I went through chemotherapy. Then I had surgery, radiation followed by targeted therapy. I kept my will-power strong during this whole treatment and came out of this disease. Now I know that even if there is cancer on your way you can remove that obstacle with the right care and treatment.

From a person who wanted to die and not go through treatment... who thought everything negative today I am transformed into a much stronger and confident person after treatment. Earlier I used to stay at home and take care of my sister and father, but now I wish to go out and do something for my country and myself. I am more hopeful towards life now.

Cancer is no longer an incurable disease. People can get treated and not necessarily die. I am a living example... I had cancer and I am alive.

I am grateful to my sister Siddiqa, who stood strong like a pillar with me and gave me the courage to fight this deadly disease. I am thankful to Dr. Meenu Walia for supporting me and giving me a second chance in life.

My experience in India was wonderful. Everyone here was so cooperative and supportive. From the hospital staff, to Dr. Meenu Walia, my neighbours where I took a place on rent. Even my maid helped me in everything by going out of her way. It is beyond expression how comfortable I felt here in an unknown land.

❑

Anatoliy Genefiko

| 64/M | CA Colon | 2017 | Tajikistan

In 2017, after doing a colonoscopy in our country, we learned about a tumour in the intestine. The doctors told us that I had cancer of the sigmoid intestine 4 stage.

For us it was a shock... the first thing we thought was that everything is over. What should I do? How and where to get treatment? Then we got to know about Max Hospital India and decided to come here for treatment. It is very difficult to describe in words how difficult that decision was, everything was difficult: a flight to another country; living in Delhi for a month and a half; a very complex operation; Chemotherapy; Finance. It was all complicated. However, I was motivated to live and be healthy again. Our doctors–Dr. Meenu Walia, Dr. Neeraj Goel and all the staff who served us, all of them helped and supported us. I am very thankful to them for this!

Max Hospital has played the most important role in our treatment process. Thanks to our doctors, I have survived. You gave us life and hope for the future. And this is the most important thing! All services rendered to us were professional and have the result.

It has been 3 years since we found out about cancer. Of course, I did not completely overcome the disease…but I would like to say that we should not despair. You have to believe. Don't lose hope. And most importantly, entrust your life to professionals, believe in your doctors.

Cancer has changed life and yes, it is really divided into before and after… Now I understand that we need to appreciate every minute of life. Be closer to each other. Love and appreciate people who are dear to us. Help those who are in the same situation. Become stronger.

❑

Bagt Ashyrova

| 56/F | CA Colon | 2018 | Turkmenistan

It was in the summer of 2018. I noticed blood in the stool and each time there was a feeling of incomplete emptying. I started to lose weight. I then consulted in my country and on the doctor's advice I had a colonoscopy in the city of Ashgabat. I was advised to take tests at an oncological centre, where I was diagnosed with colon cancer, stage 3.

Cancer came to us like a shock. When we found out that I had cancer, my whole family was very worried, nervous, spent many sleepless nights. I could not decide where to do the operation, here in Ashgabat or go to India? But then I gathered courage and in December 2018, I came to India. We met Dr. Meenu Walia, who oversaw my case at Max Patparganj Hospital, and all treatment, including surgery, were then planned. I underwent surgery and had a colostomy bag installed. In February 2019, my colostomy bag was removed, and chemotherapy was prescribed. The operation and subsequent chemotherapy took one year.

During my treatment I lost weight (9kg) because I was on a diet. After each chemotherapy I felt weak, lack of appetite, there was a feeling on the tips of my fingers as if they were frozen.

However, what boosted me and became a source of motivation for me were the stories of my acquaintances and the stories of cancer patients treated at Max Healthcare. During each visit to the hospital, I met different cancer patients with unusual medical histories, and they all spoke in detail about their path to rebirth and what turned out to be in competent hands. This was the main factor that gave me hope when I was drowning in anxiety.

I am grateful to all the doctors and hospital staff as they played the most important and key role in my cancer journey and saving my life. Before and after the operation, I received high-level medical care and never encountered any problems thanks to our conscientious translator Shivam. We are grateful to him for that. Thanks to all of them, I live in this white world. Low bow to them!

Now that I have successfully battled and overcome the life-threatening illness my outlook towards life has changed completely. Life is the only gift of fate that is given to a person once. Therefore, appreciate and love life, enjoy it. Try to stay positive and hopeful. My life has changed for the better. Morally and emotionally, I became stronger. I was once again convinced of the solidarity and courage of my family, which supported me in difficult days, helped me through this, for which I am grateful. Now I feel fit, go in for sports, yoga, and lead a healthy lifestyle.

I was fortunate that fate smiled at me and gave me another chance, and I am grateful to her.

❑

Bibiane Yomb Epse Khon

| 39/F | CA Breast | 2016 | Cameroon, Africa

I am from Cameroon, Central Africa and was under IVF treatment in my country. Later, I felt a small lump on my right breast and consulted my gynaecologist who advised me for mammography and biopsy. Doctors in Cameroon were doubtful of cancer. Hearing the word cancer, I was shocked! Doctors advised me for the removal of breast, but my family and I did not agree with their treatment plan.

After consulting many doctors in my country, I had somehow given up hope to live more because there was no proper treatment of this disease in my country and people believed that cancer is a death sentence. Later, I got the reference of Dr. Meenu Walia in India, as one of my known from my city was also treated under her and was leading her life well. They helped us with the appointment, and we came to India for treatment.

The treatment was not easy for me. I was affected physically as well as psychologically. The first chemo-cycle was very painful, and I was totally bed ridden to the extent that I was even unable to drink a cup of coffee. I lost my hair and I felt difficulties in eating and digestion but, with the support of my doctors I was able to bear all hardships.

Before coming to India for treatment, I had almost died with the advice given to me by doctors in my country. But when I met Dr. Meenu Walia, I got a new life, got a chance to live again. She motivated me very well and gave me hope to live longer. Every time she motivated me with her words that "It is curable, and you will be well very soon". I had a wonderful experience, with the staff as they were very cheerful and supportive. They always gave me a new hope with smiling face which never made me feel that I was in a hospital.

I am grateful to my family, my husband and especially my sister-in-law, who kept me motivated during my treatment. I pray to God a lot and wish for my long life. I always kept myself busy in reading the Bible. My doctor and her team helped to give me strength to fight and win the battle of cancer.

I learnt that we must always keep our hopes high. A cancer patient is also just like any other patient suffering from other diseases. I realized that life is held with a thread and that one must live every moment with great joy and resilience. But above all, always look for the right information for whichever problem you encounter.

❑

Farida Haibulloeva

| 26/F | CA Breast | 2016 | Tajikistan

I am Farida and I work as a nurse in Tajikistan. While breastfeeding my 1-year-old daughter, I felt some nodes in my right breast for the first time. Initially I ignored it, thinking it might be due to lactation and there is nothing to worry about. But after a few months, I started feeling some discomfort in my breast and discussed the matter with my husband. We started researching doctors and treatment options and consulted a gynaecologist in our country who advised me for biopsy test.

The result was positive for breast cancer and my life was totally changed. The diagnosis left me devastated, scared and numb. I was really shocked, and my life became totally black at that moment. I started crying and thinking about my small children and my family. Later with further tests I got to know that I had a stage 4 cancer. I felt hopeless and started dreaming about my death.

My husband supported me very well and prepared me for treatment. He was one who gave me both hope and healing. He was incredibly positive for my treatment and stepped ahead towards the treatment plan. I had no idea what to do, worried about my child and family. I knew my husband and children were going to follow my lead; they would deal it however I dealt with it. So, I made the decision to be strong and keep going.

Our doctors suggested to take treatment from India and with some references we reached Max Super Specialty Hospital, Patparganj, Delhi. I began my treatment with Dr. Meenu Walia. She advised for PET CT and other tests and its result gave me a new hope for life as the final diagnosis turned out to be a Stage 2 Breast cancer and found that it is treatable. Dr. Walia is truly kind and supportive and gave me a new hope to fight with cancer as other patients fought and become survivals. She planned 4 cycles of Chemotherapy, Surgery, and Radiation therapy.

I was stressed when I got to know about hair loss as a side-effect of chemotherapy and removal of my breast in surgery. I felt inferior imagining myself as a lady without hair and one breast. But my doctor counselled me that after chemotherapy hair loss stops and only required part of the breast to be removed. My family and specially my husband supported me. He always prayed to God for me and had one belief that if Allah (God) has written this trouble for us, he will also give the cure.

During chemotherapy, when I was in a state of despair, my husband took me back to good memories which we lived together and gave a preview of our future, that our children become young and start going to school/ college and now ready for marriage etc. His togetherness always made me stronger and motivated towards treatment. Now, I am under follow up, and back to my life again as I am.

Cancer treatment did not change my active life, but it did change my looks. I lost my hair and I lost weight. At first, these side effects were difficult, but I quickly learned to embrace them, and to embrace the beauty in me that cannot be taken away by medication. I wore hats and enjoyed applying make-up. A few new outfits made a big difference. I bought fake eyelashes, too. But what really mattered most when it came to coping with side effects was my attitude. I knew I could not continue to worry about what other people were thinking. I had to just deal with what was happening and face it. And it got better. Today I enjoy my full and happy life more than ever.

The lesson that I learned in my cancer journey is that we must always value every minute of our life and accept those who love and support you because we never know when bad things happen in life. I am thankful to God, that I got in touch with the right hand, on right time and at right place to get a doctor like Dr. Meenu Walia. She gave me strength and support with her guidance and gave me a new white page to write my life again.

❑

Fayzali Sharipov

| 40/M | CML | 2015 | Tajikistan

December 2015, I got sick badly in my country Tajikistan and was admitted at Cara Bolo Hospital, Dushanbe in Tajikistan.

The doctor advised me to take a course of chemotherapy, but I refused and my friend (doctor) advised me to meet Dr. Anirudh at Asan Clinic Dushanbe for consultation. Dr. Anirudh advised me to go for treatment to Max Hospital Patparganj in New Delhi, India.

December 18, 2015, I went to India, the Max Hospital staff Mr. Dileep met me at the airport and took me to the hospital. When they brought me to the hospital, I was feeling very bad, my weight was 68 kg at that time, and I realized that I had lost a lot of weight. But after getting treatment at Max Hospital, my health improved day after day. Dr. Meenu Walia cured me and I want to thank her for saving my life.

For the last 5 years I have been coming regularly to consult Dr. Meenu Walia and to get myself checked up properly. My treatment is progressing continuously and I am so thankful to Dr. Meenu Walia and team of Max Hospital.

❑

Ghaneiva Zulkhomor

| 27/F | CA Nasopharynx | 2018 | Tajikistan

I fell sick round June 2018. I had pain in my neck, so I decided to see a local doctor. Thinking it to be a seasonal problem I was prescribed antibiotics and when it pained, I took pain killers for relief. However, after some time, I developed a swelling around my neck. My nose also remained blocked for too long and I had difficulty in breathing. We consulted an oncologist, and the evaluation was in favour of cancer.

I took treatment there for a month and then my husband took me to Tashkent in Uzbekistan for another opinion and there also the doctor gave the same statement.

I was petrified, tense, and could not sleep for nights thinking about my uncertain future and my three little children. My parents and my husband all supported me a lot, yet the worries were buried deep in my heart. I stopped eating as whenever I ate, it pained in my neck. Then one day a friend of my sister who was a cancer survivor suggested that we should visit Asana Clinic where we met Dr. Anirudh.

Dr Anirudh confirmed the cancer and advised us to go to India. We came to India in November 2018 at Max Hospital and met Dr. Meenu Walia who after getting my biopsy and other tests done, started my chemotherapy. On the first day of chemo only, I had bleeding from my nose and all the pus was discharged. By the third and fourth day the swelling around my neck was gone and even my blocked nose was relieved.

After the third cycle of chemo, the results were favourable and then I went for radiation therapy for the next 7 days. All this while my husband and my mother were there with me as my support system. My doctor, Dr. Meenu Walia is an excellent doctor, very calm and composed and she knows her job very well. She gave me the right treatment and I have got positive results. She and her whole team were extremely helpful and highly professional. She explained all the side-effects of chemo and supported me emotionally when I was dealing with hair loss. Even my translators Dilip and Yash were immensely helpful and made our stay in India as comfortable as it could be.

Today, I am doing well and enjoying life with my little children. I am thankful to God and everyone at Max Hospital, especially Dr. Meenu Walia for giving me a second life.

❑

Hind Ali Sarhan

| 42/F | CA Breast | 2018 | Iraq

In the name of Allah, the most merciful, the most mercy giving! All praise to Allah whose blessing fulfils the good deeds.

The period of my illness began on 14th March 2018, when it came to notice that I have pain in my left breast. I visited the specialist doctor more than once in my country. She assured me that it is just infection in my breast and the treatment is possible with simple medicines. But she could not treat that. I repeatedly visited the doctor, but nothing changed. All I got was just a consolation as she always told that there is nothing to worry and the matter is very superficial.

After that I felt very restless and the sorrows and worries surrounded me. So, I visited the specialist once again and she ensured me through clinical examination by hands. After one week I visited her again and she then asked me to get an X-ray done. She got surprised seeing the nodes in my left breast. I recognised through the other tests that I have got breast cancer.

When I came to know that I had cancer, it was terrible news for me. My family and I was feeling very hopeless at that time. This news surprised me, and I lost the confidence in Iraqi doctors because of their laziness and carelessness.

I decided to travel outside of Qatar for treatment. I searched for the hospital which is famous for the medical services and well developed in cancer treatment, humane behaviour, and affordable price. So, I came to India and entered Max Hospital which has been selected as the best hospital for curing tumours.

Dr Geeta operated me with high expertise and deep understanding and after that I shifted under the treatment of Dr. Meenu Walia for Chemotherapy. She explained me the side-effects of chemo very well. She asked me not to get scared and supported me emotionally. Since then, she follows up my condition with professional expertise. After that I went through radiation therapy.

I finished my treatment from Dr. Meenu Walia who was cautious offering all that I required to get well with a great specialization. Until now she follows me up when I visit her. I thank all the staff, management and especially Dr. Meenu Walia and my translator Zameer Ahmad for all the support. We had heard that cancer means death and whosoever is diagnosed with it will certainly die. But today I have seen it all and I feel that nothing is impossible. I hope every person suffering from cancer gets cured.

❑

Hojiev Muhsinjon

| 23/M | CA Testis | 2020 | Tajikistan

It was 2018 and I was studying in China and leading a very active life. I was always involved in sports and was living happily imagining a settled future for myself. One day I had pain below the belt but ignored it thinking it might be because I am actively engaged in sports.

After 2 months I went to Russia and still had that pain so I decided to see a doctor there who advised me to get some tests done. The doctors told me that there is something wrong and serious and I should consult a specialist as they had not seen such a case before. I did not understand anything because the pain wasn't troubling much and was infrequent. Then I went back to my own country, Tajikistan and went to a hospital there.

The doctor told me that it seemed like the beginning of cancer. Even in Russia the doctor thought it could be cancer but wasn't sure. I got an X-ray done and cancer was confirmed. My first reaction, I did not believe that I have cancer. But next

I thought that I am not worried about myself, but I don't want my parents, my family and friends to worry about me. So, I decided not to tell anybody. After staying abroad for so long, I should have been happy returning back to my country, but I was depressed, did not go out with friends, and talked less.

I lied to my parents that I am going out on a trip and got my surgery done. The doctors told me that I need to take chemotherapy as well, so that's when I disclosed my disease to my brother and took a promise from him that we wouldn't worry and tell anything to our parents. Because in my country cancer was considered like a death sentence and people could not understand it. I took 1 cycle of chemo in my country. I did all that my doctors said and had faith in God that I would be all right. Then my brother researched and found out about Max Hospital in India from one of his friends whose uncle was treated here for his heart condition and him having travelled across the world suggested that there is no better care anywhere else than in India. So, we decided to come to India.

I decided to travel alone as both my brother and I coming together would be caused our parents to doubt. I came to India September 2020. Things were delayed because of the Coronavirus pandemic and there was a lockdown all over the world. I somehow managed to come and met Dr. Meenu Walia here who started my treatment. She planned for 3 more cycles of chemo.

Money was again a problem as I was a student and not working. I used to ask for money from my father saying I wanted to do some business here in India. He knew I was not doing anything wrong but to afford the treatment I required money frequently, so my dad was concerned so I told him about my condition and asked him to conceal it from my mother. He was shocked but then asked me to be strong and get the treatment properly without worrying about money.

All the while during my treatment I was alone in India, but my interpreters Dilip and Yash helped me immensely. They arranged for food I liked to eat. They accompanied me when I was in the hospital for the treatment. I lost my hair, Covid-19 restrictions did not allow me to travel and I used to get bored alone, towards the end of my treatment my best friend came to India to support me and started to stay with me.

Cancer has truly changed my life. Earlier I was always around my friends and enjoying myself but cancer showed me who my true people were. There were so many people whom I had helped but they did not even call or message me why I was in India for so long and I now know the real people in my life who stayed with me, prayed for me and supported me in my bad times. I value life and people better now.

Now my treatment is over, and I am cured. I am thankful to Dr. Walia, her team, the staff of Max Hospital, my best friend and above all my family for supporting me and keeping me motivated in these tough times. I believed that I would get cured and would not give up. Live every moment and have faith in God.

❑

Khakimov Khasan

| 68/M | CA Left PFF | 2015 | Tajikistan

My name is Khakimov Khasan. I was born in 1947. Before retiring I worked 48 years in different positions, but my last position was Head (Director) of trade in the town Norak.

In 2015 I had pain in my left ear and left side of neck for a long time and went to a doctor who advised to get a biopsy done. When I got the report the oncology doctors of Dushanbe told me that I had cancer in the neck.

The first thought when I was informed about my disease was "It is the end; I was going to die". I was living my life well but then this disease happened, and it took away our happiness and changed everything for my family.

I received some chemotherapy here and later was told for surgery. However, I was not very sure about the treatment. Days and nights passed with the thoughts of cancer, but I was sure I would get fine and live longer. At the start of 2016, I was informed about Indian Medicines and Max Hospital Patparganj and about Dr. Meenu Walia. Then without any doubt I came to India.

My case was handled by Dr. Meenu Walia and I was planned to undergo Chemo and Radiation therapy. It took about 18 months to take the treatment and get over this disease. During the treatment I felt support from doctors. In my life, the first place is of God and the second is for doctors like Dr. Walia. I am so grateful and thankful to the staff of Max Hospital Patparganj who are very kind, for good organization of treatment for service and their relation towards patients. Dr. Meenu Walia and Dr. Jyotika with their excellent treatment gave me new life.

The special people I thank for supporting me in my battle against cancer are firstly my family, second my doctors and third myself because I always stayed motivated to be alive, to be with family, friends and enjoy every moment of being with them.

When there was disease I did not think about next month or about plans for next year. There was only one thought "If not today, tomorrow I will die because of the disease." But now when I am successfully treated, I want to live. I feel new power and emotions for what my family is extremely glad.

When I went back to Tajikistan after getting treatment, I told everyone who had this diagnosis about Max Hospital and Dr. Meenu Walia. Once more thanks to the staff of Max Hospital, Dr. Meenu Walia, Dr. Jyotika who I wish all the best. I want them to live long and save more lives- as much as possible.

❑

Khalima Babadjanova

| 70/F | DLBCL RT Buccal Mucosa | 2018 | Uzbekistan

In Decmber 2017 my mother (Khalima) had a non-healing ulcer in her mouth. She then underwent surgery in our country and the reports revealed that she had Lymphoma.

When she came to know about her diagnosis, she did not believe it at first. She thought that there must have been some mistakes in the reports in Uzbekistan. We decided to come to India for further treatment. On March 14, 2018 I my mother and I came to India at Max Hospital.

We met Dr. Meenu Walia who explained to us about the disease and treatment. After meeting her, my mother was relieved that she was in good hands and everything would be all right.

My mother underwent chemotherapy, but it was exceedingly difficult. She was depressed, had extremely low appetite, and other side-effects like nausea, and diarrhoea after first chemotherapy. But it was bearable for the sake of treatment. It was a difficult time for my mother and family, but we made ourselves strong. We explained everything to her about the disease and prognosis. She had immense belief in God and prayed a lot that time.

The doctors and medical staff also helped us a lot. We are very thankful to Dr. Meenu Walia as she helped my mother to fight cancer. Max Hospital helped a lot in our evaluation. They had arranged translators who were always available to us. Doctors were very professional, and the operation was a great success.

Although we were in another country but the services, support from medical staff, food, accommodation and above all services of interpreter that we got here was 100 percent satisfactory. And we are grateful for them for being so attentive.

From my mother's cancer journey we all learned to live life healthily and happily. You must do whatever you want to do. Follow your passion because you do not know how short your life is. Today my mother is doing well and is healthy.

We are thankful to all the doctors, Dr. Meenu Walia, Dr. Manoj K. Johar, Dr. Sowrabh K. Arora, nurses, medical staff, and translators especially Shivam for their hard work and care for my mother. A big thanks to Dr. Meenu Walia and Max Healthcare for making our medical journey smoother.

❑

Lydia Chebet Simiyu

| 42/F | CA Left Breast | 2015 | Kenya

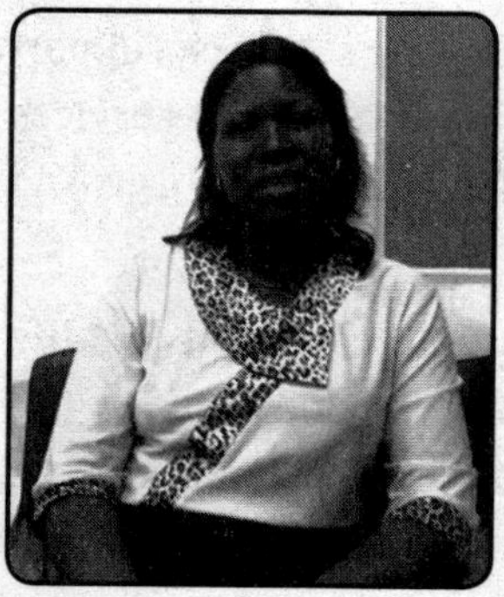

I am Lydiah Simiyu, a Kenyan citizen, and a nurse by profession. I was diagnosed with cancer back in 2013. I got my surgery done in my country, but I faced problems in getting medication. I did not have a strong financial background but then I received an international medical sponsorship and in January 2015 I came to India for medication. Here I found my doctors team headed by Dr. Meenu Walia, who is a very good doctor and a very down to earth person.

After I met her, I went through PET-CT and several other tests and started my treatment. I thought I would stay here in India for a month or two, but my disease had advanced, but the doctors here supported me and took care.

Today I am absolutely fine, there are no cancer cells in my pelvic bones. There is a very big change and a very good response towards treatment. I am doing very well indeed. I was all alone here in India, but my doctors and the hospital staff helped me a lot. They supported me mentally, physically and emotionally.

What motivated me is a young boy who is now a teenager. I prayed to God and kept my spirits high, that I will not die. I refused sickness, being bed-ridden and I encouraged myself strongly that I shall not die, but I shall live. Whenever I lost appetite, I could try new foods. I refused evil minds and whispers of the devil. I was very positive to live and be strong day by day.

True, what I thought in my mind is what revealed in my body. I was negative to the cancer in my body and I always thought that I am healed which is why I am responding well to the treatment.

Let us not take the families burdens on our mind, it kills. Some relatives discouraged me so, I moved with the positive relatives who were ready to help me and always kept positive thinking in my mind. The drugs have been strong, but I have been positive and that is why I moved towards positive healing.

❑

Makhira Begaliera

| 47/F | CA Breast | 2014 | Uzbekistan

I am Makhira and I am a practising gynaecologist in Uzbekistan. I lost my mother to breast cancer and was incredibly stressed and worried about myself as I knew about the family history of cancer. After a few days, I felt some discomfort in my breast, so I thought of going to the doctor for diagnosis on the preventive hand. Unfortunately, in July 2014, I was also diagnosed with the same caner as my mother had. As a doctor, I was aware about cancer and its treatment; so, there was nothing new for me. But after getting confirmed with cancer, I motivated myself to treat it as soon as possible. I visited Max clinic in my country, and they suggested my treatment plan in India. Taking treatment in a different country made me worry.

I mentally prepared myself for treatment in India and came to Max Patparganj, Delhi. I met Dr. Meenu Walia and she advised for Chemotherapy and surgery as a treatment plan. I got the first cycle of chemotherapy after my surgery on February 6, 2015. Despite being in an unknown land, I felt myself wonderfully comfortable and safe with Mr. Adnan, my translator. He supported me in my entire treatment journey.

When a person is diagnosed with cancer, the only thing to do is to go through it. You cannot avoid it, even though you did not cause it yourself. We all want to be strong when faced with life's challenges, but sometimes that strength is hard to access.

After going through the cancer treatment, I embrace life so much more. During treatment, I visited Taj Mahal, Jaipur and other states of India and washed my worries by collecting wonderful memories of India with me. Each birthday now is so much more than just a birthday; it is another year of life. I celebrate life. I do the things I was once afraid to do. I do not procrastinate, and I do not stop myself from pursuing what I want for silly reasons.

I specially thank Dr. Meenu Walia for supporting me so well with her professional experience. When I met her for the first time, I felt myself in the right hands. She is incredibly positive and supportive in nature. I forgot all my worries in her presence. Even the entire staff of her team was supportive and caring. Now I am on follow up of my treatment and getting a chance repeatedly to visit India with a plan to explore India more. I am back to my routine life and work with becoming a motivational example for others.

Cancer has taught me the different languages of love; that each person "speaks" their love differently. It was hard to let people help me at first, but I realized how important it was to them, and to me. Letting go and allowing others to help was a learning experience for me. Now I realize that I could not have done this without the people I love. Today I am feeling better.

It is strange to say that cancer has been a gift, but in some ways it has been. It has enabled me to understand so much more about life, about myself, and about the people I love. And now I can offer help to others making the same journey. How else would I know to tell people to plug your nose and have a candy when your port is being flushed? That advice is invaluable!

❑

Raheema Shakeer

| 49/F | CA Cervix | 2015 | Iraq

I had sudden abdominal pain and bleeding when I went to a gynaecologist in my country Iraq. She told me there is nothing to worry but my bleeding did not stop. I consulted several doctors and one advised me to get a biopsy done. Hearing about a biopsy test scared me. After some persuasion by my husband, I got the test done and the reports were positive for ovarian cancer.

I was devastated hearing the results and did not know what to do. Everything stopped around me. Then in March 2015 I had my hysterectomy done in Iraq and decided to travel to India for further treatment.

In April 2015 we came to India where I met Dr. Meenu Walia at Max Hospital and found her to be extremely wise. She advised us for some more tests. As my diagnosis was already delayed back in my country by the time, I reached India, my disease had advanced and spread despite the surgery. I was very unsure about my life, but Dr. Walia counselled us like a relative and assured me that I would be all right. We had never got such personal attention and comfort anywhere before. She planned my treatment and I received chemotherapy and radiation.

With the immense support of my husband who was always by my side during the treatment I tolerated the treatment well. I did not face any trouble in a far away distant land. All the hospital staff and Dr. Walia's team treated us so well that we always felt that we were in safe hands.

After the treatment was over, I felt much better and today it has already been more than 5 years. I visit Dr. Walia for follow-up every year and she always greets us with a charming smile. By the grace of God, I am incredibly happy and healthy. I am thankful to my husband, Dr. Walia and her team, my translator in India and Max Hospital for everything they did for me. I am grateful to God for giving me a chance to live and be happy again.

❑

Rukhshona Begakhmadova

| 33/F | CML | 2016 | Tajikistan

I had some health-related complaints and visited a gynaecologist in my country, and she advised me to get some blood tests done and then referred me to a haematologist with the reports. I was diagnosed with Leukaemia.

When I was diagnosed with cancer, I only thought about my children because they were too small. For getting treatment I left my small children back in my country and travelled far way to India. I received my treatment at Max Hospital, Patparganj under Dr. Meenu Walia.

I always motivated myself not to give up because of my family, with the help of my husband who was there with me all the time during the treatment.

I am grateful to my God that I had a chance to come here and get treatment and secondly to the staff of Max Hospital,

Department of Oncology because all of them helped us during the treatment and always motivated me not to give up. The doctors here were very experienced, especially Dr. Meenu Walia who was with me and helped me every time.

After treatment, what I understand is not to lose hope-never and never give up even if it is living with another illness. My life has changed in a better way, now I have hope and I want to live.

❑

Epilogue

Dear Reader,

As you hold this book in your blessed hands, I want you to know that you are not alone. The road you have walked, with its twists, turns, and uncertainties, is one that many have travelled before you. It is a journey that requires immense strength, courage, and resilience—qualities that I know you possess.

Throughout these pages, you have read about the remarkable stories of those who, like you, have faced the unimaginable and emerged stronger. These are not just stories of survival, but of thriving against all odds. Each of these individuals found light in the darkest moments, and so can you.

Life, with all its uncertainties, is a journey of both challenges and triumphs. It is in the face of these challenges that our true strength is revealed. Each day is a new opportunity to embrace hope, to find beauty in the smallest moments, and to realize that you are stronger than you ever imagined.

To you, dear reader, I say this: no matter where you are in your journey, know that you have within you the power to overcome. You are not defined by this disease but by your courage, your spirit, and the love that surrounds you. Believe in your strength, and never lose sight of the hope that each new day brings.

As you close this book, remember that this is not the end, but rather a new chapter in your life's story. You have the strength to write the next pages with hope, courage, and love. I am with you in spirit, cheering you on every step of the way."

With heartfelt warm wishes,

Dr. Meenu Walia

❑

About the Author

Dr Meenu Walia is a renowned Medical Oncologist in the National Capital Region of India. She has been dedicated in serving cancer patients for about three decades and continues to do so with full conviction. Currently, she spearheads the Department of Medical Oncology & Hematology at Max Super Specialty Hospital (Patparganj, Vaishali and Noida). She has the credit of being the first DNB Medical Oncologist of India attached to her name.

She started her journey as a Jr. Resident at Ram Manohar Lohia Hospital, New Delhi and today has climbed up the ladder to be the Director of Medical Oncology and Hematology at Max Super Specialty Hospital (Patparganj, Vaishali and Noida).

Dr Walia has treated more than a lakh cases over the years and being deeply involved with these patients in the most difficult phase of their life, she is a doctor who strives to bring a difference in the lives of her patients. She believes in the fact that, a doctor is not only meant to heal his patients physically, but also plays an imperative role in their psychological treatment. She is one of the very few in the country to have hands on experience in all different types of chemotherapies including HIPEC.

On her professional front, Dr Walia has a legacy par excellence. She believes in the principles of patient first and has massively contributed towards uplifting of patient care in her organization. She is a teacher for the DNB Medical Oncology students and has also been conferred the "Honorary IMA Professor" title by Indian Medical Association (IMA). She is also a reviewer of medical journals such as Journal of Indian Academy of Clinical Medicine.

She is actively involved in clinical cancer research at global level and is the principal investigator for various Global Oncology research. She is a part of 20 major international clinical trials.

She has been decorated with various awards namely Bharat Jyoti Award and Certificate of Medical Excellence by IMA multiple times. She has been awarded "Inspiring Healthcare Leaders—Dronacharya Award", by the Hon'ble Minister of State for Health & Family Welfare, Govt. Of India, Shri Ashwini Kumar Choubey. She has been conferred the "Certificate of Excellence" in recognition for the exemplary work and dedication in the field of healthcare at National Healthcare Conclave by (Late) Sh. Anant Kumar, Former Union Minister of Parliamentary Affairs.

She has been felicitated with "Bharat Vikas Parishad Shyam Bharadwaj Cancer Awareness Award 2022-23", "Inspiring Oncologist of India Award" at The Economic Times Doctor's Day Conclave 2023 by Hon'ble Deputy Chairperson of the Rajya Sabha, Shri Harivansh Narayan Singh; "ICON Award 2022" in Oncology by Dr Mahesh Sharma, Member of Parliament and Former Union Minister of State for Culture and Tourism at New Delhi.

She has also been Felicitated by the legendary Indian Cricket Mr Sunil Gavaskar at the "6th International Healthcare Awards" at Mumbai and awarded with "Life Time Achievement award" Crown Global Awards 2021 by LA Global Foundation. Her book was appreciated and felicitated by Shri R V Arlekar, the Governor of Himachal Pradesh at the Indraprastha Literature Festival.

An icon of women empowerment, she has been featured on the cover of Women's Era magazine in their special issue on Salute to the talented women, featured in "Women of Wonder" campaign by Radio Amity and Amity School of Communications. She has been felicitated with "Most Influential Women of 2021" award by Smt. Meenakshi Lekhi, Minister of State for External Affairs and National spokesperson BJP. As well as "Nari Astitva Awards 2021" - A Glorious Honor for

Exemplary Women of India by G-SIL Educational Society's philanthropic initiative Neki Ki Raah. Her profile has been featured in the "TOP 100 Influential Women of India".

She has also been Felicitated by the legendary Indian Cricket Mr Sunil Gavaskar at the **"6th International Healthcare Awards"** at Mumbai and awarded with **"Life Time Achievement award"** Crown Global Awards 2021 by LA Global Foundation. Her book was appreciated and felicitated by Shri R V Arlekar, the Governor of Himachal Pradesh at the **Indraprastha Literature Festival.**

An icon of women empowerment, she has been featured on the cover of **Women's Era magazine** in their special issue on Salute to the talented women, featured in **"Women of Wonder"** campaign by Radio Amity and Amity School of Communications. She has been felicitated with **"Most Influential Women of 2021**" award by Smt. Meenakshi Lekhi, Minister of State for External Affairs and National spokesperson BJP. As well as **"Nari Astitva Awards 2021"** - A Glorious Honor for Exemplary Women of India by G-SIL Educational Society's philanthropic initiative **Neki Ki Raah.** Her profile has been featured in the **"TOP 100 Influential Women of India".**

She has also been awarded "The Legends" at Times Healthcare Achievers Award, "The Illustrious Brands- Making India Proud" by Mail Today and also featured amongst the "9 Successful Women" by Outlook Magazine and a book titled "Luminaries in Healthcare" by India Today.

Despite being a busy practitioner in her field, Dr Walia is extremely active in working towards the welfare and supporting cancer patients, caregivers and NGOs in the field. She plays a pivotal role in inspiring cancer patients and motivating with the thoughts of cancer is curable and there is life beyond cancer. She has been instrumental in conducting various seminars and awareness lectures for patients and general public in society.

She is a founder member and actively involved in development of support groups for cancer patients, wherein the cancer survivors or the follow-up patients, help the recently diagnosed cancer patients to deal with their myths and guide them through their experiences. The group brings highly fruitful results, as the patients get a lot of motivation from the survivors.

Dr Meenu Walia is also a TEDx speaker and her talk "How to Turnaround your Cancer Journey" has motivated several cancer patients. She has authored a hugely popular self-help book amongst cancer patients and caregivers "Tips for happiness in the shadow of cancer". She has taken immense efforts in collecting highly motivating stories of cancer patients and caregivers who dealt with the disease with utmost courage, complied them in a lucidly written intriguing book. The book serves the purpose of instilling hope amongst cancer patients and help them in deal the disease. The book was translated into multiple Indian regional languages launched in 2017.

❑